"Wow," Clementine said inadequately as she stepped into sheer luxury. "This is...incredible."

The extravagance of the hotel suite was another reminder of exactly who Serge was. A rich man. Who could buy a great deal to keep himself happy. No doubt including women.

But not this woman. She needed to make that very clear to him. Somehow.

"I'm not that impressed, you know, money doesn't do it for me."

"What does do it for you, Clementine?" He was smiling at her, that big lazy Russian male smile, as if he knew something she didn't.

"Honesty," she replied, "sincerity."

The smile darkened to something else.

She'd surprised him.

LUCY ELLIS has four loves in life: books, expensive lingerie, vintage films and big gorgeous men who have to duck going through doorways. Weaving aspects of them into her fiction is the best part of being a romance writer. Lucy lives in a small cottage in the foothills outside Melbourne.

UNTOUCHED BY HIS DIAMONDS

LUCY ELLIS

~ What Every Woman Wants ~

HARLEQUIN®
entertain, enrich, inspire™

Recycling programs
for this product may
not exist in your area.

ISBN-13: 978-0-373-52886-8

UNTOUCHED BY HIS DIAMONDS

www.Harlequin.com

Printed in U.S.A.

UNTOUCHED BY
HIS DIAMONDS

CHAPTER ONE

CLEMENTINE did a double-take in front of the ornate windows, almost pressing her nose up to the glass.

Lust—that was what she was feeling. Unadulterated desire.

In the window sat her Anna Karenina fantasy. Thigh-high, fur-lined, suede Russian boots.

She told herself she was only in St Petersburg for one more day after today. She deserved something to remember it by.

Five minutes later she was standing on the worn raspberry-coloured carpet inside, sliding one stockinged foot and then the other into her dream. She felt like Cinderella trying on her glass slippers. The real test was zipping them up above her knees. She was six feet tall and her legs held much of her height. She had shape to them. She had shape to all of her.

She almost gave a whoop of delight when the boots zipped up a treat.

The girl kneeling before her lifted the flaps. 'They can go higher. Shall we try?'

She spoke English, but in these luxury stores everybody did.

Without hesitation Clementine hitched up her burgundy leather skirt, feeling slightly naughty as she flashed her suspenders. She reached down and pulled the fur-lined suede up and up, to kiss the fleshy curve of her inner thigh.

Her legs looked impossibly long with the leather skirt

clinging to her hips. Absorbed in her own reflection, she slung out a leg and stroked the fur meditatively. Out of the corner of her eye she caught a flash of movement behind her in the mirror, and looked up to collide with the gaze of a man standing by the door.

He wasn't idling in the doorway, lurking. He was purposefully filling the space. Announcing his presence up front. Owning it.

And he was looking right at her.

He had to have a head of height on her, and he was built to go with it, and Clementine would bet her last pair of designer knickers on that size being one hundred per cent lean muscle.

He was quite a sight. They didn't make men like that any more.

Maybe they had in earlier centuries, when Russian men went into battle with muskets, or even earlier when they needed to club things and skin animals to feed their families. Oh, yes, she could imagine him half naked and marked by claw-marks across his back and chest, bestriding the steppes. In fact—she nibbled her bottom lip—she could imagine that quite vividly.

But nowadays, in an age of technology and convenience and the liberation of women, you just didn't need men like this any more.

Except in bed. An unexpected flush of warmth moved through her body.

Imagine if he laid his hands on you.

Imagine if it was him adjusting the tops of your boots.

Her eyes flicked to the mirror and registered that the Cossack hadn't shifted an inch, but instinctively she just knew he'd moved some muscles because the look on his face mirrored her own: unadulterated fascination. With her. Male, down-and-dirty fascination. As if she was his own personal little sex show.

Clementine felt his eyes on her like a slow burn, sliding straight up the inside of her bare, exposed leg. It was that good, and almost as tantalising as being touched.

She should cover herself up, but after a year of keeping herself nice she was enjoying the attention. It was harmless. If this guy wanted to look, let him look. It wasn't as if he *could* put his hands on her. They were strangers. It was a public place. She was safe.

She was enjoying it.

She bent down, nice and slow, folding over one fur flap to reveal the length of her bare upper thigh and then the other. Then she ever so slowly tugged down the leather bunched at her hips and lengthened her skirt, inch by inch, as she had seen so many models do for the camera, until she was decently covered.

There. Show over.

Time to pay for the beauties, head back to the rats' nest where she was staying and catch up on some sleep. Except when she looked back at the mirror the Cossack was still there, holding up the world on those big shoulders. He'd folded his arms and Clementine registered powerful muscle under the strain of his jacket.

Her pulse leapt. He was every woman's fantasy, and also a little bit scary—not only because of his size. With his clear intent she got the absolute impression he was waiting for her.

A shivering awareness ran through her body like an electrical shock, but she got herself moving, fumbling with her handbag as she dug out the equivalent cost of her meals for the rest of the week to pay for the boots.

'You have an admirer,' said the girl, boxing up her old shoes with a discreet glance in the direction of the door.

'Probably a shoe fetishist,' murmured Clementine, but there was a smile on her lips as she said it.

Inhaling a deep breath, she swung round and headed

for the exit—only to discover he wasn't there. She actually dropped a step, idling for a moment in the doorway, disappointed.

She emerged into the street and swung her designer bag as she headed south—and that was when she spotted him. Leaning against a limo, thumbs in designer pockets, running a gaze over her that sped up and slowed down depending on which part of her body he got hooked on. Clementine lost a breath and then her heartbeat raced.

Okay, Clementine, walk on, she lectured herself. *There's no way you're going over there and introducing yourself.* Guys dressed like that with limos on tap were not territory she wished to stray into. She'd already had her brush with his type. Never again. The industry she worked in was rife with women who cashed in on their desirability for a certain lifestyle. She wasn't one of them, and she wasn't starting now.

Serge fastened on the sway of her hips as she walked away, flashing those sensational thighs showcased by fur and sheer stockings. He knew what was holding those stockings up: delicate midnight-blue suspenders.

He had been leaving the jeweller Krassinsky's, where he'd left his father's wedding cufflinks to be repaired, and crossing the art nouveau atrium that linked several high-end stores in this building when he had spotted her through the shop's entrance.

A young woman bent at the waist, a leather skirt hiked up around her hips, as comfortable in the middle of the shop as if it had been her boudoir, her shapely bottom encased in burgundy leather, swaying provocatively. He'd seen two strips of pale flesh before the lacy tops of her stockings took over, attached to delicate suspenders.

It had ground him to a standstill.

When she'd started tugging up those boots lust had flashed through him like a lightning strike.

If she'd stopped there he might have dragged himself away, but all of a sudden she'd hooked out a leg and he'd got an eyeful of her inner thigh—that soft, fleshy curve at the very top of a woman's leg, pressed into prominence by the clasp of the stockings clinging to her legs. Serge had swallowed hard as she'd begun smoothing the fur right up to that spot.

That's the girl—a bit higher...very nice.

As if hearing his thoughts she'd lifted her head and met his gaze in the freestanding mirror. She'd frozen. Her face was heart-shaped, her mouth wide, her chin pointed. Despite the clothes, despite the pose, despite the lashings of make-up, she looked as if butter wouldn't melt in her mouth. He had waited for her reaction and been rewarded by a small private smile, and then she'd bent and slowly peeled the fur down to expose the tops of her thighs. To him.

Because it had all been for him. She'd known he was watching her.

Which had made it incredibly hot.

As her skirt had slithered down he'd known he'd be thinking not only about that spot at the top of her left thigh but also about her smile for the rest of his day.

He'd watched the girl switch her attention to the salesgirl—no longer his little show but simply a woman making a purchase—and it had chastened him. This wasn't Amsterdam. She wasn't on the market and she wasn't his type. The hooker look had never interested him, and whatever frisson she had got from the experience was over.

He'd left her to it, but as he'd handed his bag over to his driver he'd found himself lingering by the car, just waiting to see her emerge. Curious, interested.

She stepped out of the building in those ridiculous boots and above the revving of his libido he got the full impact of a fifties pin-up come to life. Lustrous golden-brown hair, narrow shoulders, full breasts, curvaceous hips and a lick of a waist. Her legs were strong and shapely and went on and on. And on.

The realist inside him told him he should let her go. He had places to be, and it wasn't as if he couldn't find another woman to warm his bed.

Then she moved and he forgot about every plan he had for the rest of the day.

He knew the moment she noticed him. Her lashes dropped, screened her eyes, and she just took off, those sensational legs in those infamous boots eating up the pavement. Her leather skirt twitched provocatively over the bounce of her heart-shaped bottom. She'd be gone in a few minutes, lost in the late-afternoon crowd.

As if sensing his indecision, she chose that moment to turn her head over one pretty shoulder and give him a smile Mona Lisa would have envied. Subtle, but it was there. *Come and get me.*

Then she was off with a swish of her long hair.

Serge propelled himself away from the car, and with a brusque instruction to his driver to follow took off after her.

Clementine hadn't been able to help herself. She'd cast a last look over her shoulder, and when she'd seen his gaze was still glued to her she'd smiled. Apparently that was enough—because now he was coming after her.

Instinctively she sped up, her whole body tightening with anticipation.

When she checked again he was still there, impossible to miss, taller than anyone else, a big, insanely gorgeous man, with chestnut hair falling carelessly over his temples, curling at the base of his broad neck. In the bright sunshine she could see the faint shadow of where he'd shaved, and the square cut of his chin and the sheer bravado of his grin as he caught her looking.

She shouldn't be encouraging this. She should turn around on this crowded street and confront him. But she didn't. She slowed down. She put a little more sway in her hips and kept walking.

She checked again. He was clocking her, but not closing in. She felt relatively safe.

Serge pulled back his pace momentarily as Boots turned out of the Nevsky, watched her cross against the schizophrenic traffic, earning a few hoots and screeching tyres from drivers—probably more at the sight of those long legs than any traffic infringement.

She had a real energy in her body that translated into the sexiest walk he had ever seen on a woman. And what struck him was the fact that she seemed utterly oblivious to the chaos she caused around her.

He didn't want to lose her.

Clementine risked another glance over her shoulder but she couldn't see him. Disappointment slowed her walk, prosaic reality returning with every step. Game over. Damn.

Up ahead was the underpass. She hated those mucky tunnels, never felt completely safe, but it was the only route she knew. The boots were starting to rub, and without the distraction of her ridiculous sexual fantasy the worries of the day began to crowd into her mind.

Serge stood at the kerb and watched as she began to descend into the underpass on her own. He saw the danger closing in around her at the same moment, and without another thought launched into a run.

Bozhe, this woman took chances. She'd known he was on

her tail, and now two men were honing in on her bag, flapping on that lavish hip, and she just kept walking, lost in her own little world.

She shouldn't be let out on her own. The thought briefly crossed his mind before the more savage *Take them down* intruded and he lunged into the underpass, aiming at the guy who was already reaching for the strap of her bag.

He grabbed her assailant by the scuff of his neck and dragged him off.

It was satisfying to use his body for something other than sitting in a plane and a car. He was fit—boxing and running took care of that—but to fight was in his blood and he hadn't had one in many years.

Not that it was proving much of a challenge. The first assailant launched a fist that he blocked.

Instead of acting smart and getting the hell out of the way, Boots was launching an attack of her own with her bag, smacking it with gusto into the back of the head of the guy nearest her.

She distracted him and the first guy got in a lucky punch, grazing his face. Fast was best, and Serge slugged him one, then zeroed in on the second thug who moved fast, snatching the bag she was flapping around as if it was a club.

At least she wasn't stupid. She let go, and the guy started running. The one on the ground crawled to his feet and took off, leaving Serge flexing his knuckles and alone with Boots.

'You let him go!' She was standing there in that short skirt, looking outraged.

At him.

Serge shrugged, rubbing his abused jaw. He didn't feel like explaining that beating both men to a pulp was the only way he could have kept them there, and that her safety had been foremost in his mind. Instead he opted for the more obvious standby. 'Are you all right?'

'They took my bag!' she wailed.

Foreign. British? Her voice was pitched low, slightly husky.

'You're lucky that's all they took,' he answered her in English. 'These underpasses aren't safe. If you'd read your guidebook, *moya krasavitsa*, you'd know that.'

She looked at him with clear grey eyes full of reproach.

'So it's my fault, is it?'

She had her hands on her hips now, stretching that white satin blouse across her breasts until the buttons strained. *Bozhe*, there was black lace under the white. This girl seemed incapable of keeping her clothes on. She was a walking incitement to the male libido. What did she expect was going to happen to her if she went around dressed like this?

Bizarrely, he wanted to tear off his jacket and wrap it around her—which would just ruin his view.

She wasn't quite what he'd expected up close. She was better, but in a less upfront, more feminine way, and the longer he looked at her the more other things began to leap out besides the obvious. Up close she was younger than he had imagined—closer to twenty than thirty. It was all that make-up. She didn't need it. Her skin was luscious, like a ripe peach.

She swore creatively, pushing the fringe off her forehead. 'What am I going to do?' she said fiercely.

He had the answer to that, but he would wait for her to suggest it.

Hands still firmly on her hips, she walked a few steps in the other direction, then turned and met his eyes properly for the first time. Some of the agitation had left her, and she turned up a face more interesting than conventionally attractive. She had thick brown eyelashes and clear grey eyes and a dappling of freckles across her nose.

She really was lovely.

'I'm sorry,' she said earnestly. 'I've been very rude to you.

Thanks for scaring them off. You didn't have to, but it was a nice thing to do.'

He hadn't expected that—or her sincerity. He shrugged it off. He didn't need to get sentimental about picking up a girl in downtown St Petersburg. He only had to drop his gaze ever so slightly to remind himself she wasn't a shrinking violet.

'Don't men look after women where you come from, *kisa*?'

'I imagine they do.' She gave an awkward shrug, then another one of those little smiles of hers. 'Just not me. But thanks again.'

With that she took off, the slender heels on those boots clicking on the cobbles. She held out her arms stiffly from her body, as if balancing herself, a gesture that reminded him she had experienced a nasty shock.

He couldn't believe she was walking away.

Damn. 'Hold up.'

She looked over her shoulder.

'Can I give you a lift somewhere?'

She hesitated, looked at him with those doe eyes, and said, 'No, I don't think so. But thanks, Slugger,' and damn well kept walking.

Click, click, click.

CHAPTER TWO

GODDAMN. Unbelievable...

Clementine hobbled over a puddle, heading towards the light at the end of the underpass, cursing under her breath. She tried to focus on the practicalities. She would have to find the embassy. She would have to borrow money from her friend Luke. She would have to phone her bank in London. She would do it all once she'd had a little sit-down and a cry.

Her handbag was her lifeline.

It was her own fault. She was usually much more street smart than this. She'd been so wrapped up in her little fantasy with the Cossack she hadn't been paying attention. She'd ruined that too. She'd been too shaken, too tongue-tied to do anything more than try to block him out whilst she extricated herself from the situation even after he'd rushed in to save her.

Her chest gave a little flutter at that thought. He'd been magnificent. He'd just handled it. You didn't run into guys like that in London.

The light hit her face and, pulling awkwardly at her skirt, she ascended the steps. She was chilled despite the sun, and that was her own fault too. She should have changed out of this ridiculous outfit Verado liked her to wear, back into her street clothes. But there hadn't been time, and she'd left the bag of clothes at the store, and now she was wandering the streets of St Petersburg in great boots but frankly looking a little too uncovered for her own liking.

Emerging into the street, she hobbled over to a nearby kiosk and took a seat. She was really shivering now, and it didn't have much to do with her lack of layers. She supposed it was delayed shock, but she also felt naked without her bag—vulnerable. She was used to depending on herself and that bag had everything she needed to keep herself safe. She was beginning to wish she hadn't sent the Cossack away.

It was useless going back to her lodgings. She needed to head back into the city centre, find Luke.

That was when she saw the limo. It was idling across the road, one of its doors angled wide, and then she saw him, striding straight towards her. He'd removed his jacket and had his hands shoved into his pockets, so that the fabric of his superfine blue shirt pulled taut across a muscular chest and abdomen. Clementine's miserable thoughts dwindled to a virtual halt. He looked powerful and it wasn't just his size. It was the way he held himself, with tremendous confidence and that measured response to what was going on around him she had seen in action in the underpass.

But what he was giving her now was full sensual male interest. Clementine told herself she could handle men, but all her female instincts were telling her she couldn't handle *this* man at all.

He was so male as to be of another species.

Big shoulders, big arms, hard thighs—long and lean and coming straight at her.

He'd crunched bones for her, broken skin, shed blood.

'Come on, get in. I'll take you wherever you want to go.' He spoke abruptly, his voice deep and deliberate.

She just sat there, looking up, trying to clamber over the overwhelmed feeling to something more considered.

He lifted those big hands of his. 'I'm a good guy. I don't wish you any harm. You need some help, yes?'

'Yes,' Clementine said softly, distracted by the intensity of his green eyes.

'Are you staying far from here?'

Clementine knew she should tell him nothing and refuse the ride. But he had helped her. He had put himself at risk for a stranger. This *was* a good guy. This was a very, very sexy man. This would buy her a little more time with him. And she was so tired of looking after herself. It wouldn't hurt to accept a lift.

'Do you know where the Australian embassy is?'

'I'll find it.'

And she believed he would.

Serge gave directions to his driver, watched as those long legs folded themselves into his car, slid in alongside her, observed her scoot over to put a respectable distance between them. Then she shifted forward and leant down.

She was unzipping the boots.

The shell of each boot collapsed and she tugged one stockinged foot out, then the other, revealing her long legs in those sheer pale stockings that gleamed like silk. Her activity seemed unselfconscious, as if he couldn't possibly be interested, but of course she had to know what she was doing. She wriggled her toes and cocked a curious look at him up through her lashes.

'Sorry, honey,' she said. 'They're new, and they're rubbing.'

She pressed her knees primly together and folded her hands in her lap, utterly ladylike.

She was incredible.

'You're Australian? From Sydney?' His own voice sounded

hoarse, and he gave an inward laugh at his susceptibility to this woman.

'Melbourne.' She smiled, her eyes not quite meeting his. It was such a subtle smile. She kept her lips pursed, as if she was keeping a secret.

If only she'd stop rubbing her knees together. The *shub-shub* of the fabric was highly stimulating to his imagination.

'So far away. What are you doing in Petersburg? Business or pleasure?'

'Both. I'm here working.' She gave a little shrug as if it wasn't important. Those lips parted into a more open smile. 'But I've dreamed of seeing St Petersburg. It's so romantic, so full of history.'

'You like what you've seen so far?'

'Very much.' She gave him a sidelong look, making it clear she wasn't talking about the city—and didn't that just notch up the temperature in the car? She turned her head away, made a show of looking out of the window, exposing the length of her lovely pale throat, and he dwelt on the golden tendrils of silky hair tickling against her neck.

He decided to cut to the chase. 'When do you leave?'

She met his gaze, let him see those grey eyes, darker now than when he had first seen them. 'My contract winds up tomorrow.'

Two days. Perfect. 'Such a shame,' he mused.

'What do you do?' she ventured. 'I mean, you must do something—you're riding around in a limo.' She laughed nervously. 'You're either rich or something else.'

He laughed low, and watched the pulse in her throat give a little throb. 'Or something else,' he murmured, which clearly intrigued her.

'You're not one of those overnight millionaires you read about, are you, honey?'

'*Nyet*, sorry to disappoint you. I worked very hard for my first million.'

'Right.' Those slender hands fluttered in her lap. She was obviously attracted to him, but the money helped. His inner cynic gave a rueful shrug.

'This would be the moment to ask you, if you're not otherwise engaged, to join me for dinner tonight.'

He actually saw her swallow. She moistened her lower lip, dragging his attention to the contours of her mouth. She looked at him through her lashes. 'You work fast. I'll give you that.'

'You haven't given me much time.'

'Oh, I can't imagine that stopping you.'

'Nothing much does, *kisa*.'

She gave a negligent little shrug, a naughty sparkle in her grey eyes. 'Okay, Slugger, we'll see how you do.'

A challenge—and didn't he just relish that?

Lifting his head above the pleasure horizon, he made a quick judgement call. This girl clearly liked to play games, however guarded she was being now. It was reasonable to wonder how many other men she'd played them with.

He hesitated.

Did it matter?

This was his favourite type of female. A woman with a sparkle in her eyes and a willingness to just enjoy herself. No ties, no drama. No happy-ever-afters.

This girl was clearly that woman.

Libido humming nicely, he gave her body a comprehensive, less polite once-over. In response she surprised him. Her hands knotted up in her lap and her shoulders tensed. That little Mona Lisa smile flickered and vanished. She turned the lights down low on her eyes with those thick lashes.

Chastened, he put a clamp on his imagination.

It was a reminder that he needed to be kind and considerate and gentlemanly—as he would be with any other woman.

And look after her until she waved goodbye in a few days' time.

She was going on a date with the Cossack.

Clementine's imagination was beginning to gallop, but before it did perhaps she should take the opportunity to clear a few things up. But what was she going to say? *I don't make a practice of putting on sex shows for strange men? I've agreed to dinner but that's it. I'm a nice girl.*

But he *had* asked her to dinner, hadn't he?

And he'd rescued her.

That was huge. She was still feeling a little breathless over that.

And, honestly, how nice a girl *was* she?

He really should be rewarded.

A little smile formed on her lips.

She needed to think this through. She'd seen the way he'd looked her over, as if making a sexual inventory of the bits he'd like. She knew which way this road led and she didn't want to walk it again. Not even for a Cossack whose incredible green eyes made her tremble behind the knees and her nipples perk up.

He had one arm spread along the top of the seat, so that his hand hung just inches from her shoulder. He had positioned himself so he was angled towards her, long muscular legs stretched out. Without his jacket she could see the hard width of his shoulders and the taut flat belly delineated by the fitted dark blue shirt, crisp on his large frame. He really was mouthwateringly delicious.

For crying out loud—she had to stop this now! She didn't even know his name, or he hers. She could remedy that, at least.

'I'm Clementine Chevalier, by the way,' she said, sticking out her hand in a forthright fashion.

'Clementine.' His accent did wonderful things to her name. He took her hand and lifted it to his lips, and she felt the tingle all through her girly bits as he turned her endeavour to keep their interaction on a guy-to-guy basis into an old-fashioned gesture. The sort of gesture that got her just where her inner princess lived.

'I am Serge—Serge Marinov.' *Serj*, she pronounced silently, practised it a couple of times. It was far too sexy. She was such a goner.

Expectation shimmered in the air. The car had glided to a halt. Clementine registered belatedly that they were no longer moving and hit ground level as real life intruded again. She reached for her boots.

'Thanks for the lift.' She sounded breathless even to her own ears. 'Should I give you my address or shall I meet you somewhere…?' She trailed off.

'I will collect you,' he said, as if this was the only logical response, 'and I think you should let me handle the embassy.'

Okay. She wasn't going to argue over that. 'You really want this date,' she observed as he opened her door, helped her out.

He gave her an inscrutable smile. 'How am I doing?'

'How do you think?' She threw a feminine sway into her hips and preceded him into the building, enjoying herself far too much.

People were looking at them.

Probably wondering what a girl like her was doing with a guy like him.

She was wondering the same thing.

Clementine had pictured queues, waiting endlessly, forms to be filled in. Apparently Serge Marinov didn't live in that world. He lived in a parallel universe where you were taken upstairs to a plush office and offered tea or coffee or something stronger, and where a senior official turned up in a neat business suit and low heels, eyes lighting up as she focussed on Serge. The woman was so poised and elegant, her flirtatiousness pitch perfectly low-key, giving Clementine a sick feeling in the pit of her stomach. She knew women must fawn over him all the time.

Yet he had saved her from who knew what in that underpass, and he'd asked her out to dinner, and now he was making a difficult situation evaporate. He was putting in all the work. And within an astonishing half an hour Clementine was sorted: passport, visa, bank account. All of it done and dusted.

'Who on earth *are* you?' she blurted out as they descended the marble stairs of the embassy building. It was shabby and worn, but the interior had clearly once been a beautiful example of early nineteenth-century classicism. In any other situation she would have lingered to take it all in, but right now all she was interested in was the man beside her.

'I have a few contacts in the city,' he answered neutrally. 'Where can I take you now?'

Anywhere you want, a little voice sang. The boring, nice middle-class girl part of her gave him her address, registered his disapproval.

'Is it too far out of your way?'

'It's not a particularly savoury area.'

'I'm sure your car will be all right—I mean you can just drop me and go.'

That stopped him in his tracks. 'I am concerned that a woman is living alone in this building. Who arranged this for you?'

'It's a work thing.' Clementine shrugged, feeling uncomfortable under his scrutiny. She put her game face back on. 'It's fine, really. I'm a big girl, Serge.'

It was the first time she had said his name and it ran through her like electricity. He seemed to like it too, because he was suddenly idling in front of her, blocking her view of the reception area and the street with his body. She liked it that she could barely see over his shoulder, even in her heels.

He seemed to read her thoughts, because he leaned in a little closer and said softly, 'You seem much too lovely to be staying there on your own.'

Clementine felt the backs of her knees give. She found her gaze buzzing on the line of his mouth. It was so unforgiving, yet there was a softness in his lower lip. She wanted to press her thumb there, see if she could coax a smile out of him. Just for her.

'You sure know how to sweet-talk a girl,' she said, as lightly as she could, but her voice came out a whole octave lower.

He leant in, his breath soft on her ear. 'Do you need sweet-talking?'

'A little,' she demurred, the sudden rush of response in her body embarrassing her.

He gave her a slow, knowing smile. 'I'll keep it in mind.'

This date wasn't just about dinner. She'd been a little slow on that score. Already she'd been planning her dress, and imagining candlelight and waiters bringing champagne and being romanced, when she should probably be thinking about lingerie and condoms.

It was stupid to feel disappointed. He was here now and all of this had started because of sex. And he expected it was going to end with sex. She was a big girl. She understood how it all worked. She'd learned the hard way that guys like this didn't date working girls like her with a view to a future. But she needed to make a decision about how she was going to handle that before she went any further.

Not that he'd pushed anything. Apart from that brief gesture of his lips on her hand he had not laid a finger on her. He was all well-mannered restraint. She felt completely safe with him, and enormously grateful, and suddenly horribly self-conscious—because all of a sudden she wondered if he looked at her and saw what another man had seen in her unhappy past: a sure thing.

The Vassiliev Building. He wouldn't kennel a dog there. Yet this warm, vibrant girl was sleeping there. Probably with a lock on the door a five-year-old could snap.

If there were no funds she should be staying in one of those concrete hotels that housed tourists. They weren't attractive but at least they were safe. Well, this was the last time she'd be sleeping here, so that problem was solved.

It still went against the grain to let her out here, and Serge found himself accompanying her inside and up the stairwell. She seemed embarrassed, as if the dire surroundings were somehow her fault.

She'd been quiet on the drive across town from the embassy. He'd expected a little flirting, but she'd gone back to pinning her knees together and she hadn't taken off her boots. The mixed messages didn't bother him as much as watching her let herself into that room and knowing he was going to leave her there.

She was unbelievably trusting. She had climbed into his car. She had given him her details. She'd probably open this door to anyone.

'Keep this locked,' he said, thumping the doorjamb with the side of his fist. 'Don't open the door to anyone you don't know.'

She had sort of angled the door so he couldn't see inside. Either that or she was worried he was going to lunge at her now they were in stepping distance of a bed. Which didn't make sense. She'd been more in danger of that in the back of the limo. But he had no intention of rushing anything. A few hours wasn't going to make much difference, and he intended to work Clementine Chevalier over so thoroughly she wouldn't forget St Petersburg in a hurry.

It was going to be very mutually enjoyable.

If she stopped giving him these glimpses of vulnerability and expectation. As if simple consideration was something she hadn't much experience of.

He handed her his card. 'This is my number. Call me if you have any hassles. I'll be here at eight.'

She nodded, those grey eyes wary in her heart-shaped face. Then that sweet curve at the corner of her mouth made its appearance, and Serge fought free of an impulse to lean in and kiss her—because once he did that he'd be setting up a softer scenario than the one he had planned.

Straight up sex, not seduction. That was on the menu for tonight and tomorrow night.

He'd save the seducing for a woman who needed it.

CHAPTER THREE

CLEMENTINE lingered in her shabby rats' hole long enough to whip off her boots and slip on jeans and her trainers, then hightail it for the Grand Hotel Europe.

'You're doing *what*?' Luke slid his spectacles down to the end of his nose after listening to her story.

That those glasses were only for show made the gesture all the more endearing. They had known each other since Clementine's teenage years, when Luke had moved in next door. Meeting up with him again in a pub in London had been serendipitous. Without Luke, Clementine doubted she would have lasted more than a few months in London in that first year. He'd got her this job with the Ward Agency.

Clementine sat down on the end of his hotel bed. As head of public relations for the Verado shoot Luke got a whole room in the Grand Hotel Europe.

'It's just dinner, Luke.'

'No, he ogled you in a shoe store and followed you up the Nevsky—'

'And saved me.'

'Saved you—right.' Luke was all cynicism. 'Some guy stole your bag—'

'Two—two pretty nasty types. And then he just made the whole problem go away. Took me around in his limo.'

'Just you make sure that's all it is. Dinner.'

Clementine blew air up her fringe. 'Yes, Mum.'

Luke sat down beside her on the end of the bed. 'Sweetie, this guy isn't the one.'

'What one?'

'The one you're looking for.'

'I'm not—'

'Hey, Clem, remember who you're talking to. I was there last year, remember? To pick up the pieces. This guy is rich, right? Impressive? It sounds familiar to me. You're his type, darl, but he's not yours.'

No, she wasn't going to believe that. She wasn't going to let one bad experience alter the course of her life. But she had, hadn't she? And with Luke's reminder reality began to seep in fast. 'I don't know what's going to happen, but I really want to find out.' She could feel her face heating up.

Luke shook his head. 'I'm going to give you my mobile, okay? You ring me here at any hour. Wherever he takes you, you make sure you get the address, and if he wants to take you anywhere out of the city you say no—got it?'

'He's not a serial killer.'

'Probably not, but he knows you're a tourist. I can't believe you let some strange man ogle you in public.' But his blue eyes were twinkling. 'Those legs of yours should be insured.'

'They're not that good.' Clementine gave her thighs a pinch.

'They're sensational, princess. Now, listen to Uncle Luke—are you packing protection?'

Clementine blinked.

'Hell, Clem, I know you haven't been dating for a while, but nothing's changed, love.'

'Never rely on the guy,' intoned Clementine, wondering what Luke would say if he knew she'd never had casual sex in her life.

'Good girl.' Luke's expression softened. 'But you're not going to sleep with him, are you?'

Clementine went for an insouciant shrug, and Luke threw back his head and laughed. 'I'd love to be a fly on the wall when this bloke realises he's going home alone.'

'Maybe he just wants to get to know me better.'

Luke squeezed her knee. 'You go on thinking that, darl, and one day pigs will fly, my flirty little puritan.'

Puritan. Hardly.

She dated. Just not in the last twelve months. But mostly she worked. She'd been working from the age of seventeen, supporting herself in any number of menial jobs, studying at night school. It didn't leave a lot of time for relationships. Even friendships. She had loads of acquaintances—it went with her job—but only a couple of real friends. She knew the difference—just as she knew this date with Serge Marinov was a bit of fun to celebrate the end of her contract with Verado. She would flirt herself silly, and fantasise about what it would be like to be with a guy like this, and then—Cinderella-fashion—vanish at midnight.

Which reminded her... She retrieved Luke's condoms from her clutch bag and tossed them onto the nightstand.

She only did relationship sex, whatever Luke might think.

Given the circumstances of their meeting, she tossed aside her pile of short skirts and tight tops and took out the pale green satin dress she had packed for evenings out with her co-workers. On the hanger it looked plain, but once her curves had filled it, the wide belt cinching in her waist, it was something else.

Not that she was complaining about the curves. She couldn't help the way she was shaped, and despite all the good and bad attention it got her she wasn't going to waste her youth hiding behind acres of fabric. The pleated bodice covered up her chest modestly enough, and fastened in a halter around her neck, leaving what she considered her best feature—her shoulders—bare.

She wound her hair into a chignon and highlighted her mouth with deep pink lipstick, then slipped on her favourite strappy gold sandals.

From the window she saw a low-slung silver sports car enter the courtyard. It had to be him. She didn't want him coming up here again. It was too intimate, and it created a bit of a power imbalance she wasn't comfortable with.

There was an elevator in the building, but the concierge had advised her not to use it. She teetered a bit on her heels as she reached the bottom of the stairwell, and then she saw him striding towards her. She registered the moment he saw her—and that she had literally stopped him in his tracks.

'Hi,' she said, a tad breathlessly.

He wore tailored trousers, the shirt open at his throat was expensive, and the dark jacket screamed money. He was so physically imposing she ground to a halt. He didn't take his eyes off her, and there was nothing friendly in the look he gave her. For a moment all she saw was a flare of almost feral wildness in those beautiful Tartar features but then he was pulling it back, hooding his green eyes and covering the ground between them in a few steps.

Oh, Lord, she was toast.

Clementine drew her little clutch up to her waist, bent her elbows in a classic expectant pose, and waited for him.

'You look breathtaking.' His deep voice held the same appreciation she saw in his eyes, and for a giddy moment she thought he might bend to kiss her. But he merely reached for her elbow to guide her.

He looked so good—radiated such strength and confidence. What was it about this man that sent the blood thrumming through her body? It was all wrong, because this couldn't be anything more than dinner.

It was a lot more than dinner. If he could, he would have driven her straight to his place and set aside the 'getting to know you' niceties.

He couldn't help but admire her ability at sliding into a low-slung car. She had it down to an art form. Like much else. He watched her do it with only a slight hitching of her skirt and acknowledged she'd probably had lots of practice. Women like this required high performance cars—it came along with the body she had on offer, and Clementine was a piece of strategically engineered female design straight off the make-me-a-bombshell factory floor.

And he had her exactly where he wanted her.

He shut the door with an expensive-sounding *snuck*.

In under a minute he was beside her, his hand throwing the car into gear, taking in a discreet scan of that body.

'Ready?'

'As I'll ever be.'

Was she nervous? A little thrown by that thought, he let the motor throb and she actually jumped.

'Do it again,' she encouraged.

Smiling at her enjoyment, he reversed back towards the road with the expertise he'd built up with this car, aware he was showing off. He made a mental note. She liked the car. She liked surprises.

Then she opened her mouth and trotted out that cute little accent.

'So, where are we going, Slugger?'

'There's a place on the Neva I think you'll enjoy.'

He didn't want to take his eyes off her. How had he forgotten how much of a bombshell she was?

'This is an incredible car,' she commented.

'You like fast cars, *kisa*?'

She gave a little shrug. 'I guess. I like the rush.'

'I can open it up on the highway, but it's a no-go in the centre of the city.' He flicked a glance over her recumbent body. 'Why don't you sit back and relax and enjoy the ride?'

'I will.'

She had angled her body so that one leg was tucked behind the other, showcasing the long shapely line of her body from shoulder to breast and then to the luxurious curve of her hip and down her long, long legs to the clasp of her strappy shoes.

She was watching him; he could feel her curious gaze all over him. He almost growled as she said, 'I like the red leather. It looks expensive.'

They'd hit a snag in traffic, and instead of looking for a way out of it he leaned back and followed the length of her slender arm, the curve of her breast, lifted his eyes to the smile on her lips. Her eyes were gleaming mischief at him.

Everything about her told him she was practised at being provocative, but her smile and the look in her eyes spoke of the fun she was having with it.

'You like expensive things, *kisa*?'

'I really like it that you're rich,' she answered, batting those false eyelashes at him outrageously.

'And I really like a woman who appreciates leather. I liked your skirt this afternoon.'

'It's nice against my skin.' Her cheeks were starting to turn pink.

He had to ask. 'What else do you like against your skin?'

She laughed—that husky sound again. 'Warmth.' She suddenly sounded more down to earth. 'I get cold easily.'

'Good to know. I'll make it my responsibility tonight to keep you from getting cold.'

'You'll loan me your jacket?' Her eyes were sparkling. Her little smile had blossomed. 'Such a gentleman.'

He gave her a look, then a second look—as if to check and see that what he'd seen the first time hadn't altered—and then his eyes went all speculative. Male speculation.

Clementine drew herself together and settled back a little further in her seat. Maybe it was time to rein in the flirting.

She concentrated on the traffic outside, telling herself she could handle this guy. He asked her a few light questions about her time in St Petersburg and the atmosphere in the car settled down.

Feeling a little more confident, she covertly ran her gaze down the length of him. From his unruly close-cropped hair to the high planes of his face that revealed a southern Russian ancestry, the sensual jut of his mouth, the clean, solid lines of his jaw, down the strong column of his throat to his big husky body that made her cheeks burn. He was a sight to incite a female riot.

He looked at her again, and his eyes told her he knew exactly what she was doing.

Deciding to brazen it out, she said outright, 'I like your jacket.'

He smiled, forming appealing creases around his mouth that made him appear younger, more relaxed, as if he was enjoying her company. He got the joke. He'd play nice. She found she could relax.

The traffic eased as they went over the bridge. One of his hands rested lightly on the wheel, the other throwing gears as he negotiated the car in and out of snags and got them across town with a skill that mesmerised her.

Other images began to crowd her head and it was difficult to censor them. The way he had lunged at those men—all that aggression and cracking of bone—the way he had taken physical blows for her and scared those guys off. He'd done it because underneath all the *politesse* and courtesy he had shown her he was a big, strong, rough guy—and didn't it make all the girly parts of her tingle? She'd been on the money the first moment she saw him. They just didn't make men like this any more.

'You've gone quiet,' he said, in that deep, gravelly voice.

Pulling herself together, she slammed down the reply that was on her lips. *I was admiring the view.*

It really was time to pull the curtains on the flirting. She was having so much fun; it was like the old days, before she'd learned how her teasing could be misconstrued.

'I was thinking how light it is.'

'The White Nights are almost upon us. There's nothing quite like them.'

'It's a shame I won't be here to see them. But it's lovely right now. The light seems to mellow everything.'

He glanced at her. 'I find that too.'

She was something else, Serge reflected as he followed the twitch of her seductively rounded bottom into the restaurant. She was built the way women used to be, before diets and gyms and size zero. She was shaped this way because that was how nature had made her.

Mother Nature had done a superlative job.

He'd decided on an out-of-the-way place—small, cosy. There was a chance Clementine wouldn't like it. He'd brought a couple of women here before, watched them pick their way through the traditional Russian cuisine, listened to them dismiss their surroundings as *quaint*. But he was only in town for a couple of nights, and he loved the place. It was family run and noisy, and after eight there were gypsies.

Tonight wasn't about the location. It was merely a means to an end. But he wondered now why he had instantly thought of Kaminski's in relation to Clementine.

She was with him because she liked the money; she'd been pretty upfront about that with all her little flirty comments.

Correspondingly, his feelings about this girl were down and dirty and basic. He had what she wanted, and she *definitely* had what he was after. Where he took her for dinner shouldn't figure into it.

Clementine tipped her head back as he escorted her inside, taking in the low-beamed ceiling. She scanned the room, already filled to capacity with diners. The décor was simple—round tables, wooden floors, murals of historical Russian scenes on the walls. He wondered what she thought of it.

She beamed at him. 'This is amazing. You are a dark horse. I expected a wine bar.'

The pleasure on her face took him off guard. Men's heads turned as they weaved between the tables and he felt an unfamiliar trickle of possessiveness.

Clementine seemed oblivious, giving him little backward glances over her shoulder as the restaurant's owner, Igor Kaminski, led them to their table. It brought back his uncharacteristic pursuit of her up the Nevsky, and fancifully he acknowledged that despite corralling her into a dinner date nothing had changed. She was still a step ahead, as elusive as ever, and he was enjoying it.

She gave an exclamation of delight as they reached their table, and he observed Igor grow about a foot as he gave her a potted history of the restaurant. Then she did that thing all women did as he seated her, smoothing her hands over her lavish hips and thighs to adjust her skirt. Somehow Clementine managed to turn it into a performance of female sensual pleasure. Igor stood there, a big smile on his broad, unhandsome face, watching her.

Am I supposed to hit him or order? Serge wondered, only half amused. He broke the spell by asking Clementine what she would like to drink.

She gave him one of those sweet little smiles. 'I'll leave it up to you.'

He ordered Georgian wine, and Igor returned with the menus himself, flanked by three men Serge knew were his sons. Clementine was enjoying herself, so he sat back and let the good-natured teasing unroll as *zakouski* was served and the men encouraged Clementine to taste—pickled mushrooms dipped in sour cream, different varieties of caviar, *ikra* fresh from the Caspian, salty *sevruga*. She washed it down with a mouthful of her wine, and Serge observed her trying to make sense of the heavily accented English, giving everyone equal attention.

Their table was busy in a noisy restaurant. This wasn't what he had pictured doing tonight. Food, alcohol, a little sweet-talking and Clementine gasping his name for a few enjoyable hours had been the plan.

Then Clementine leaned towards him and said, 'When does our date start, Slugger?'

Serge beckoned Igor over, whilst not taking his eyes off her, and murmured something to the owner. Their company evaporated, leaving them alone.

'Everyone's so friendly,' she confided over the rim of her glass. 'They certainly know you.'

'I think, *kisa*, the drawcard is you,' he observed wryly.

'Don't be silly.' As she slid her spoon through her soup her eyes teased him.

The little red candles in the glass bowls on the table between them cast a tantalising glow over her heart-shaped face. Her lightly tanned bare skin—what he could see of it—had the burnish of pale honey, extending from the curve of her shoulders, the slender length of her arms all the way down to those long-fingered hands and the gold bangles that clinked around her wrists.

A girl who looked like this, with the level of independence Clementine exhibited, knew exactly what she was doing. She had to know what tonight was all about. She was going home on Saturday, which meant it had to be tonight or tomorrow.

The anticipation was beginning to burn.

'So, what is it that brings you here, Clementine?' He needed to do his bit—the what-do-you-do, tell-me-your-story routine—before the food and alcohol kicked in and he put thoughts of a soft mattress and his hard body into that pretty head of hers.

'Is it time to get to know one another?' she teased, wishing her tummy wasn't fluttering. She'd done this before— flirting in a public place. But it didn't feel public. It felt very, very intimate. Maybe too intimate for a first date.

He leaned towards her. 'Only if you want to, *kisa*.'

His eyes made her so aware of herself she was sure she was blushing. Trying to get back on track, she decided to fire some questions of her own at him.

'So you're a regular?'

'When I'm in town.'

'A different girl every time?'

'I've been known to drop in alone,' he replied, noticing the way her index finger had stopped drifting up and down the stem of her glass and she was gripping it now. What was the problem? Different girls? Did she need a little reassurance that he didn't make a habit of picking up women off the street?

Actually, this was a first—but he didn't want to draw attention to it, remind her they had only met this afternoon. For all her free and easy vibe, he was getting the distinct impression Clementine was more than capable of putting the brakes on this.

'So, tell me why you're in Petersburg?' He needed to distract her.

'I'm here for Verado—the Italian luxury goods company.'

'*Da*, I know them.'

'They're doing a promotion for their flagship store on the Nevsky. That's me—PR girl.'

Serge sat back, absorbing her pride in her job. PR. Of course. What else would a girl like this do but charm and influence people for a living?

'The grand opening is tomorrow night and then it's all over. Back to London.'

Serge had lost interest in her job. He was much more interested in the different lights he could see in her hair—golds and reds and browns. Was it natural? Probably not.

'I imagine you're very good at public relations?'

'I guess I am. I like people.' She noticed he was paying more attention to looking her over and it flustered her. 'I'm not that keen on Verado—all very old-world sexist misogynist management—but it's my job to make them look good, so I do what I can.'

Serge was tempted to comment that the fleapit she was currently inhabiting told him more about her job than words. Instead he said, 'What else do you do, Clementine, besides influence people?'

'Do you really want to know?'

There was something in the way she asked, angling up her chin but with a hint of vulnerability in her eyes. He hadn't expected that.

'Yeah, I do,' he said, surprising himself.

She gave him a curious look he couldn't read. 'Truthfully, not much lately. All I seem to do is work.'

'You're a beautiful woman. No serious boyfriend?'

She met his eyes candidly. 'I wouldn't be out with you if I had.'

Serge lounged back, rolling his shoulders, all big lazy Russian male.

Honestly, thought Clementine, what *was* it about men and competition?

He sipped his brandy, his eyes warm on her face, her bare shoulders.

'What about you?' She tossed back her hair, giving him her hundred-watt smile. 'Why isn't a rich, gorgeous guy like you taken?'

'Gorgeous?' He looked amused. 'Good to know I measure up, *kisa.*'

He hadn't answered the question. Clementine's smile faded. Okay, it didn't mean he was married or had a girlfriend or anything.

'So no one's waiting up for you at home?' The question sounded so gauche she could have kicked herself.

'No.' He settled his glass on the table. 'No one.'

It bothered her. He studied her suddenly tense face intently. 'What gave you the idea I was married?'

'A girl can't be too careful,' she said lightly.

Da, he could imagine an endless stream of guys hitting on her. Married men. Single. Hell, gay men. Any man with a pulse.

He had a personal distaste for adultery. He didn't fool around with married women, ever. So why in the hell did it annoy him so much that she had brought it up?

It was the idea of a married man making a play for her.

Any man.

Because he wanted her. For himself. Exclusively.

And why in the hell did he feel that at any moment she could get up, excuse herself from the table and never come back?

Clementine knew there was something about her that attracted guys like this. Good-looking, confident men, who thought they could bulldoze her into bed. And they always had money. Luke said it was her personality, but he meant her confidence. She was a girl who liked to dress up and flirt. She always had. She intimidated a lot of nice guys who were too scared to approach her, imagining every night of her week was booked, or who—like Serge—wanted to know why she wasn't in a relationship.

She had been. In two short-lived unsatisfactory relationships with nice guys who in the end had bored her silly. She recognised now that they had made her feel less like herself and more like the girl she imagined she should be. Clementine with the lights turned down.

Serge watched the emotions flickering across Clementine's expressive face. Her guarded eyes suddenly made him feel uncomfortable with his crass plan for a couple of nights' entertainment.

'You still haven't told me what you do,' she said, sitting back.

She genuinely wanted to get to know him, and something tightened up in his chest.

'I'm in sports management,' he replied, unease making him brief.

'Is it interesting?'

'Sometimes.'

Clementine's heart sank. He didn't want to share any information about himself with her. For a moment she was thrown back to that strange whirlwind of months, almost a year ago, when she had been pursued by another wealthy man who had dodged personal questions as he smothered her in unprecedented romantic attention.

After her last break-up she had gone back to dating casually—until Joe Carnegie. She had met him through one of her PR jobs and he'd been a client—which meant he was off-limits by her own personal code. But the minute the job was done he'd been on the phone, roses had been delivered to her door. He had encouraged her to play up to her 'gifts', as he'd called them, supplying her with spectacular dresses he could show her off in. They would arrive boxed before a date. He had groomed her for a role and she had let him.

She had been so naive.

He'd wined her and dined her and treated her like a princess. She had opened herself up to him so quickly, so easily. Until the evening he'd taken her to a swish restaurant, the night she had decided their relationship should move beyond the bedroom door, and presented her with a real estate portfolio. He had purchased her a flat—a place he could visit her whilst he was in town.

It had never been about her. It had been all about the way she looked on his arm and how well she would perform in his bed. And then it had got worse. A couple of days later she had read in the newspaper about his engagement to a French pop star, who was also the daughter of a leading industrialist. A woman from his own social strata. She had been something else all along. He had always intended her to be his mistress on the side.

The memory still burned. He'd done a job on her and she was still paying the price. She had told herself she wasn't going to let it ruin tonight, but already she was second-guessing Serge's motives. He had been nothing but a gentleman—but so too had Joe Carnegie. She'd already come to the conclusion long ago that she wasn't very good at working men out.

She looked around the restaurant, with its ambient lights and the laughter of other patrons and the wonderful smells of old-style Russian food, and realised she'd landed in yet another one of her stupid romantic fantasies.

'Excuse me,' she said abruptly, shifting to her feet. Serge rose. 'Powder room,' she murmured, unable to look at him.

The mirror in the ladies' reflected back her pale made-up face and she cursed her lavish use of the mascara wand, because those tears prickling in her eyes were going to leave tracks.

She wasn't sad. She was damn angry. With herself.

How in the hell did she get herself into these situations? Did she have 'sucker' tattooed on her forehead?

Two other women joined her at the taps, and Clementine made a show of washing her hands, checking her hair.

She looked up and recognised one of the girls as their waitress—one of the Kaminski daughters.

'Serge Marinov,' said the girl, making a sizzle gesture. 'Lucky you.'

Yes, lucky me. Clementine gave her dress a tug and shook her head at her reflection. She was being an idiot. She had an incredible man sitting out there in that restaurant, waiting for her, and she was hiding in the ladies' loo because one time some other guy had measured her value as low. It was time to suck it up and get on with her life. She was calling the shots, and if Serge Marinov had some stupid male agenda—well, she had one of her own.

As she approached the table he caught sight of her, and something akin to relief washed over his face.

Clementine almost ground to a halt. Well, fancy that. Guess who was on the hop. Confidence lifted her spine. He stood up as she approached, and she smiled to herself as he seated her.

'Miss me?' She couldn't resist the question.

'Every minute, *kisa.*'

'Are we still eating?'

'Coffee?'

'Tea.'

When the samovar came the gypsy entertainment had invaded the restaurant and it became impossible to be heard above the music.

Serge watched Clementine coming under the spell of the

performance, finding himself baffled by her. As the restaurant erupted into clapping she joined in, humming along unselfconsciously. When the performers came round to collect gold coins she fumbled in her clutch bag.

He reached across and laid a stilling hand on hers, tossed some money into the skirts of the girl.

Clementine shook a finger at him. 'I can pay my way, Mr Millionaire.'

'You're with me,' he replied, as if that said everything.

Clementine's inner princess sighed, but her capable independent outer working girl patted his arm. 'Come on, rich guy—let's get out of here and I'll buy you an ice cream.'

There was a flurry as they left. Clementine had made an impression on the Kaminskis, which was fine, but next time he came in here without her there were going to be questions. She was that sort of girl.

Hell, he had his own questions. Nothing had gone to plan. He should be rushing her across town right now to his place, after a meal spent trading sexual banter. Instead he'd spent the evening watching her enjoy herself—except for that bizarre moment he'd thought she'd got up and left the restaurant.

Walked out on him.

Even now he wanted to take her hand, weld her to his side, but she kept a neat distance between their bodies, held onto her purse with both hands, that classic little pose of hers complementing the sway in her walk.

Although it was after ten the evening was still light. They were so close to the White Nights of June. Serge shrugged off his jacket as they strolled down towards the embankment. The urge to slide an arm around her was very strong but he reined it in. Somehow this had turned into a real date. A first date.

Clementine looked up at him. 'Thank you for inviting me. All I've been doing lately is working. It's nice to put on a frock and be taken out somewhere fun.'

Bozhe, she was so sincere. And he was buying it. It probably made him a sap, but there was something about her in this moment that made him want to believe her.

'You're a very easy woman to please, *kisa*,' he said at last, 'but the evening has hardly begun, no?'

Clementine hid a smile. 'Maybe for you, Slugger, but I'm beat and I've got an early start tomorrow.'

And didn't that just tie up all his expectations in knots and toss them in the river? Serge rolled his shoulders. 'Right,' he said—and everything fell into place.

She'd known all along tonight wasn't going to end in bed, which meant the little act in the car had been for her own amusement. He remembered the sparkle in her eyes, the invitation to laugh along with her.

He'd missed it because he'd been deep down in lust land.

Which meant tonight was a lost opportunity—for both of them. She was going home on Saturday, leaving him with a decision to make.

Was she worth the pursuit? Or—the better question—should he be messing with her? This nice girl? All sweet and sincere? And didn't that just get him in the traditional Russian male part of himself that he didn't make a habit of showing off? Where had he got the idea she wouldn't need seducing? Why *shouldn't* she make him work for it?

Instincts he didn't have a whole lot of familiarity with told him he needed to handle this delicately. Another, more familiar instinct was telling him to take her in his arms and drive every thought she could possibly have about other men out of her head—at least until tomorrow. It had to be tomorrow. Because she was going back to London on Saturday.

And if he didn't have her in his arms in one form or another tonight he was going to go crazy.

He reached and caught her hand—something he'd been wanting to do all night. She turned towards him, expression expectant, amused. He closed the space between them and lifted his other hand to hook one of her artfully liberated coils of hair away from her cheek. Her smile faded, her eyes grew a little rounder, her mouth softened.

'You're killing me, Clementine,' he said in Russian, and moved in to put himself out of his misery.

In that moment she made a soft little sound of dismay and to his surprise turned away, slipping her hand free of his with a nervous laugh.

'I still want to buy you that ice cream,' she said over her shoulder.

Ice cream. Not sex. Not even a kiss. Not tonight.

She began walking, swaying a little on those silly heels, and he stood there, stock still, gazing after her.

She threw him a backward glance.

'Coming, Slugger?'

She was going the wrong way. The ice cream vendors were in the other direction. But her question dissolved into a teasing smile, and without giving it a second thought he took off after her.

CHAPTER FOUR

SERGE had spent the morning listening to the argument that had broken out between the president of his company and the man he trusted above all others: trainer Mick Forster. Broadcast from the boardroom in the Marinov Building in New York City to the screen facing him, it had convinced him of one thing.

'I'll be at JFK tomorrow lunchtime,' he said briefly, and closed his laptop. He pushed away from the desk, striding over to the windows of his Fontanka Canal apartment.

He'd been out of the country less than a day and he already had problems with a young fighter, Kolcek, who was up on assault charges and getting a raft of publicity that was not the kind the organisation needed. More importantly they were behind on the stadium going up in New York—an ongoing issue—but his management team were scrambling in the onslaught of media attention, as evidenced by this morning.

He didn't like the look of it.

Yet all he could think about was that because of tardy contractors and a coked-up fighter who needed to be cut loose he was going to lose Clementine Chevalier.

Sexy, tempting, guarded Clementine. What *was* her game?

He'd taken her back to that dismal lodging last night, insisted on walking her up to her door. He'd been thinking more about the woeful security than infiltrating her defences when he'd lingered in her doorway. He'd seen once more the drab room, and then his eyes had lit on the condoms sitting on her bedside table right beside the door.

For a girl who didn't kiss on a first date she had come prepared.

Was she sleeping with someone else? Was that the problem?

She'd said she didn't have a boyfriend, but that didn't mean she wasn't sexually active. In fact it would be a crime against nature if she wasn't.

Except right now he only wanted her sexually active with *him*.

He acknowledged he'd been unusually disappointed by the discovery she wasn't quite what she seemed. For a few hours there he'd been enjoying the fantasy: man and woman out on a date, the simplicity and honesty of their interaction. Yet when it came down to it he would have left it there last night. Nice girls didn't feature in his personal life.

He wasn't in the market for a wife, or even a significant other, if that was the phrase, and the girl Clementine had seemed to be for a while there would have expected the whole romantic package.

He didn't do romance. He did sex.

And what a girl like Clementine was offering in all her luscious glory was clearly uncomplicated, sizzling sex. Oblivion between her lush thighs. The promise in those sparkling eyes at the beginning of the night. The complete lack of emotional ties a girl like that came with. The sort of girl who could be bought.

A former lover had once accused him of being cold-blooded, but he doubted that. It was why he picked his partners very carefully. Women to whom under no circumstances he would become attached. Women who liked what he could give them more than anything he might promise for the future.

He had seen what emotional attachments could do—the mess they created, the havoc they played with innocent lives. He had seen it played out in his parents' lives.

His father had loved his mother completely—taking over her life, turning all of their lives into a twopenny opera. When he'd died Serge had been ten years old and his mother had been devastated. Barely able to cope. He had seen both the intensity of love and the chaos it wrought when it went awry, or was simply taken away. His mother had remarried for financial reasons. Her second husband had beaten her for seven long years before she'd taken a familiar way out with an overdose of pills.

He had been away at boarding school, and later in the military. He had known nothing of her life until he'd stood by her grave with distant relatives who had spent no little time filling him in on the details of her disastrous second marriage—details no one had seen fit to give him during her sad life.

Emotional detachment came easily to him.

So last night, when Clementine had seen the direction of his gaze and blood-red colour had risen up to the roots of her hair, he had been curious to see how she would play it. She had kept her cool and stared him down. Before babbling. He had to go now. She had his number. He had hers. Maybe he could call next time he was in London.

At first he'd thought she was giving him the brush-off. He couldn't remember the last time that had happened to him. This gorgeous, sexy, clever girl who wanted him to believe she had the morals of a nun, or next to it, was handing him his walking papers.

Then it had all made sense. She had put the ball in his court—was waiting to be asked to see him again. His body was saying yes but his mind had gone stone-cold. Something about the entire scenario: foreign girl in a cheap hotel, holding back on any sexual contact, waiting for him to make this about more than a one-night encounter.

He hadn't been born yesterday. It wasn't going to happen.

He'd had no choice but to leave without making any definite plans with her, but as he had walked away down the dank, dimly lit corridor he'd glanced back and found she was peeking out into the hallway, drawing back as he caught her and closing the door.

And that was that.

Except he was still thinking about her after a conference call, an hour looking at complicated design plans and a lot of coffee. He hadn't slept well. Sexual frustration could do that. He'd had two cold showers—one on arriving home and another first thing this morning. There were other women he could call, but it was Clementine he was interested in.

He swigged another mouthful of coffee.

Where was she now? Working her little job? PR for Verado. He knew Giovanni Verado. High-end masculine luxury goods. She'd meet a lot of men in that job. Men with money—which was probably the point.

The nice girl had evaporated around about the time he'd spotted those prophylactics. If she wasn't sleeping with *him* on a first date, she was sleeping with someone—or planning to.

His mouth twisted cynically. She liked the money. She probably had several guys with the right cars, the right lifestyle on a string and she was working it. Girls who looked like Clementine, with that level of independence and confidence, were never single. There was always something going on.

Yet there was something else about her.

He could still hear her husky laughter, see her clapping her hands, singing along with the music last night although she didn't know the words and it was a foreign language to her. He remembered how she had been dismayed by his attempt to kiss her and then covered it up.

He wanted to phone her and hear her voice. He wanted to see her. More basically he wanted those long legs wrapped around him and her little sounds of pleasure urging him on.

But he was going to New York and time was what he didn't have. She'd said something about a launch tonight. He could turn up, try his luck.

A wry smile touched his mouth. Life wasn't about luck. It was about going after what you wanted with single-minded determination and not stopping until you had it. In business and personally.

No, better to ring and arrange to meet up with her. He didn't want to give her much choice, and in the flesh, in broad daylight, he'd be a little more persuasive than he'd been last night. He'd respected her boundaries but it hadn't got him far. He hadn't turned a single gym into a billion-dollar business without knowing when to push.

Clementine settled at a pavement table, thanking the waiter who brought her a coffee. Across the road was the Verado flagship store, where she'd spent the morning and most of this last week. She'd agreed to meet Serge at this café because of its proximity to work.

When she'd heard his voice a couple of hours ago her whole world had ground to a halt. She'd drifted away from the group she was talking to and said breathlessly, 'Serge,' and literally heard his intake of breath. His voice had been pitched lower then, darkly seductive in its accented rumble. She'd closed her eyes just listening to it, lost in the sensual spell.

She really hadn't thought he would call.

But he had, and now she was waiting for him because he wanted to see her, speak to her, probably organise a second date. He'd have to be quick. Her plane flew out at four tomorrow morning. He was keen, though. Barely twelve hours had passed since they'd said goodnight.

He might ask her to stay a little longer, and a big part of her was considering saying yes—oh, hell, yes.

Imagining she had lost him last night had made her a little more reckless than usual this morning. She had lain awake going over every minute of their date, isolating everything that told her Serge was nothing like Joe Carnegie. All of her instincts told her he was a good guy. He hadn't pushed when it had been clear enough he had hoped for more. She wasn't going to read anything into that. All men wanted more. It was just some could be obnoxious about it.

What bothered her was that she had let Joe Carnegie come between them at a crucial moment. She had wanted to kiss Serge last night but fear had held her back. Fear of it only being some sort of sexual conquest on his part, of opening herself up to another man only to have her sensibilities ripped apart. It was only a kiss, she reminded herself, but she had never felt so strongly attracted to a man in her life, and she needed to be sure before she went any further.

Thinking about it now, she tried not to have any regrets. Serge hadn't walked away, and this morning he wanted to see her. He was keen. He liked her. He was making an effort.

Except he was late.

She glanced at her little watch, with its pretty diamond-studded face. She had bought it for herself soon after she'd landed the job with Verado. Most people had parents or significant others to help mark special occasions like that. A psychologist friend had told her it was important that when you didn't have those mainstays in your life to make an effort to look after yourself, and so she had. And every morning when she slipped it onto her wrist she felt she was taking care of herself.

I'll give him another five minutes, she told herself. He's only a quarter of an hour late. Maybe it was traffic. But definitely five minutes. Maybe at a stretch ten…

'Hello, beautiful girl.'

He was idling in front of her table, all height and muscles and testosterone. She took in the jeans, white T-shirt, brown leather jacket. He was freshly shaved, hair tousled, energy rolling off him in waves. Clementine didn't look at him so much as collide with his deep green Tartar eyes, and her heart began to do a thuddy thing that made it hard to hear over the pounding of blood in her ears.

'Oh, hi.' She endeavoured to sound casual.

He gestured abruptly to the waiter. 'What would you like to eat, *kisa*?'

'Oh, I can't stay,' said Clementine, getting herself together. 'I'm supposed to be at my job, and you're late, so I can only give you five minutes.'

He dragged a chair up close to her and straddled it. As he dropped in front of her she gave an involuntary jump. His sudden physical proximity made it very difficult to hold her ground and her first instinct was to retreat back in her chair. He smiled knowingly, as if her reticence was exactly what he was after.

'Give me five minutes, then.'

Unaccountably she flashed back to how last night had ended. Even now her cheeks grew warm as she remembered Luke's condoms, like neon signs pulsing on her bedside table. He probably hadn't thought anything of it, but she had blushed, and he'd certainly seen that, and she had spent last night tossing and turning—convinced he'd seen through her to the gauche girl she sometimes felt herself still to be. That was before Joe Carnegie had torn the scales from her eyes.

He was studying her face, her pink cheeks, lingering on her mouth. 'You are a gorgeous woman, Clementine.'

She'd been told that before, although it wasn't strictly true. She was far from being a beauty. Her nose was slightly too long, her chin a little pointed, and she had too many freckles…

'Am I?' She made herself hold his gaze. 'Is that what you came to tell me?'

'I haven't stopped thinking about you.'

Oh, she liked that. 'I'm flattered.'

His eyes were knowing, full of promise. They were playing some sort of game, she recognised, except she didn't know the rules.

'I've got a proposal for you, *kisa*.'

Clementine gave an internal sigh of relief. Mentally she began shifting her entire afternoon. Surely she could carve out a few hours before the launch, when all the work had been done, and she *had* planned to take a nap and get ready for the evening.

She really, *really* wanted to spend more time with him.

Serge studied her expectant expression and the rest of her, liking what he saw. She was all dressed up this morning, in a dark blue suit, but managed by dint of the pinched waist of her jacket and the cling of her pencil skirt to look outrageously sexy. In a classy sort of way. This look played havoc with his hormones in a way the tight leather skirt hadn't. He liked her all covered up. It made it more of a challenge to imagine what was underneath.

Well, here went nothing.

'I've got to fly to New York City tomorrow on business, I'd like you to come with me.'

Clementine felt as if she'd been slammed at speed into a wall.

'I'm staying in the penthouse suite at the Four Seasons for a week. I think you'd enjoy yourself, Clementine—a little pampering, some nice restaurants, buying you some pretty dresses, see a show…me.'

Him. Clementine felt sick. She was thrust back in time to

Joe's smooth delivery as she had bleated across the table at him, 'But I don't want you to buy me a place to live. Anyway, I have a place to live.' And he'd frowned and told her he wasn't spending his free time in London shagging her in a shared flat.

That brutal. And that fast she'd lost all her girlish illusions. The next morning the newspaper had shredded her self-respect.

'I understand it's presumptuous, but I need to be there, and I think we have something, Clementine. I'd like to explore that.'

She picked herself up and brushed herself off. 'Would you?' Her voice came out like a shard of ice.

It was happening all over again.

He was offering her stuff as if she were for sale. As if her body was for sale. Because *come with me to New York City, baby* wasn't an invitation to enjoy his hospitality without serving herself up to him on a plate.

More fool her.

All she'd wanted was a date. A chance to spend some more time with him, get to know him. All of it hopelessly naive.

Right in front of her was the reason she had tried to settle down with boys who didn't push, who weren't driven by their libidos—nice, gentle guys who in the end left her cold. Men like Serge were the other end of the spectrum—exciting, challenging, but fuelled by testosterone, confident in their ability to run the world on their own terms and by extension run her.

Well, she was running in the other direction. She'd learned her lesson. She wasn't some rich man's plaything.

She stood up so abruptly her chair almost toppled over onto the pavement. 'That's quite an offer, Serge, but I think you've got the wrong girl,' she said hotly.

He was on his feet, not looking so sure of himself now. She could actually see him thinking. Probably working out which girl was next on his list to invite for a little nookie in New York. God, men could make you feel like crap.

'Clem?'

She turned as Luke's hands closed around her upper arms.

'Are you okay, babe?' He was looking Serge up and down. 'Have you upset her, mate?'

Given any other situation, Luke's suddenly aggressive stance in support of her would have been amusing. It was kind of like a meerkat standing up to a Siberian tiger.

Serge's gaze had narrowed on Luke's hands, and she couldn't believe what she was witnessing. Did he actually think she now belonged to him? One date and her body was his to ship off to his penthouse for his use? Was he going to take on Luke? Because she didn't think her gentle friend was going to come off pretty face intact!

She shook her head at Luke. 'It's all fine, sweetie. Let's get back.' She cast Serge a frosty look. 'I'm finished here.'

Serge went cold. *What in the hell had just happened?*

Had he not been explicit enough in everything he'd offered her? It was a very lucrative deal over and above the sex. What was going on? Was she holding out for something else?

Okay, maybe he'd been a little cocky about it. But he'd been so convinced she'd say yes.

She'd said no. *Had* she said no?

And now she was with this metrosexual guy who was bristling like a guard dog at him.

As if he'd ever hurt a woman in his life. Suddenly what had seemed simple and straightforward felt like a huge mistake.

'I have your answer, Clementine,' he said formally. 'Forgive me if I've offended you. It wasn't meant that way.' He wasn't going to stand there and pressure her in this thug role he was beginning to feel he'd been cast in. 'Enjoy the rest of your stay.'

His good manners welded Clementine to the spot. All of a sudden the last few minutes seemed to have rolled up into a ball of confusion in her head. Maybe he hadn't propositioned her. Maybe it was up-front an offer to spend time with him— his best effort to fit her into his schedule. She knew all about seventy-hour weeks. He said he had business in New York City. It wasn't a pleasure trip for him. Maybe he just wanted to get to know her...

Had she read him wrongly? Was it just an innocent invitation from a very busy man?

Suddenly the entire world seemed to narrow down to that pinprick of vision she had fastened on the spread of Serge's muscular shoulders as he walked away.

Was she really never going to see him again?

You'll never meet anyone like him again, a little voice whispered in her head. You knew that yesterday—the moment you clapped eyes on him. You knew that he was special. You knew he had been made especially for you. He was your fantasy come to life.

And maybe you're his. Maybe he's feeling exactly the way you do and you've said those terrible things to him and you're never going to see him again.

What had she done?

What had she done?

Her feet were moving. She could see him a long way from her now. She wanted to run but it wouldn't be any use. She could see him getting into his car. She opened her mouth to call out to him but her throat had closed up, and then she just stopped, dead in the middle of the pavement, as his sports car swiftly rejoined the traffic.

She still had Luke's mobile. She had Serge's number. She began rummaging in her bag. What would she say to him?

I've changed my mind. I want to come. I want to see where this leads me...where you lead me...

'Clem.' Luke had caught up with her. 'What is it, darl? What's going on?'

It was the reality of Luke's voice and the memories that came back with it that had her dropping the phone back into her bag, the frenzy of feeling subsiding. Luke had helped pick up the pieces when the Joe Carnegie incident had exploded in her face. She had slept in his and his partner Phineas's spare room for a week, and he had cared for her with all the kindness and tenderness she had never found in any of the guys she'd dated.

Serge Marinov was no different. She'd imagined him as her hero come to life, but her history told her the odds were against it ever working out.

Her best friend Luke was a reminder that she deserved more.

It wasn't in her nature to mope. There was work to do, and she was kept busy all afternoon sweet-talking the snooty representative of a high-profile fashion magazine who had been housed in the Grand Hotel Europe instead of the Astoria Hotel.

Try the Vassiliev Building, she thought, even as she twittered on about the incredible history of the Grand Hotel. The painful irony being she only had those stories because Serge had told them to her on their magical date. She must have been convincing because the woman, mollified, agreed to a larger suite in the hotel.

I can do this, she thought, walking through the lobby. She was spending the night with Luke, unable to face even one more night in the fleapit. Her dress was upstairs and she intended to take a long hot shower.

She had a party to go to. Parties she could do. It was men she had a problem with.

As she stepped into the elevator one of the species gave her a covert once-over and she narrowed her eyes, mean as a dunked cat.

She was still feeling prickly as she moved through the crowd at the launch. The fashion show didn't go smoothly, but it was the hiccups that made it fun. The models galloped down the runway—pretty boys carting luggage, wearing watches, flashing cocky grins at the cameras. Clementine did her usual meet-and-greet, brain switched off, dress switched on. She loved this black velvet evening gown. It was elegant and flattering, and Verado had loaned her a string of diamonds to wear around her neck. She was a walking advertisement tonight, and it suited her down to the ground. She was good at her job and it correspondingly made her feel good about herself.

If men thought she could be bought maybe it was time to start asserting her financial independence. She earned a reasonable living. She just had an expensive clothing habit. But she was twenty-five years old. It was time to stop living like a teenager and start looking towards her future. The fairytale husband and three children might never materialise—and given her romantic history and today's disaster it felt further away than ever. She needed to look after herself. Protect herself. And that meant settling into her career.

She was turning from one group of buyers to cross the floor to another when she saw him.

Six and a half feet of Russian male wasn't easy to miss. He was all dressed up in a tux, his unruly hair tamed. He looked devastating, a powerful man among many lesser men, and for a moment in time she merely stared. Until she recognised the older gentleman he was speaking to was Giovanni Verado himself.

Verado was a notorious womaniser. Probably swapping

notes, she thought snappily. But in her heart she knew it wasn't true. Serge had been nothing but up-front with her, and she kept replaying his expression when she had thrown his invitation back in his face. He'd actually looked baffled.

But why was he here? He knew this was her job. She'd certainly blabbed all about it last night, revealing more than she was comfortable with now. She'd said some indiscreet things about Verado. Serge hadn't mentioned a connection to the owner. Serge hadn't said much of anything that was personal.

Her mouth suddenly felt very dry, her palms moist.

It didn't fit the character of the man she believed she knew to drop her in it. Why would he? Why would Verado care about her opinions as long as she did her job?

No, what was worrying her was that she suddenly realised she knew nothing about him other than the fact he made her senses whirl every time he looked at her, and she'd felt so safe and admired in his company.

Right now her heart was leaping into her mouth because he'd come, and it couldn't possibly be a coincidence.

He'd come for her.

A rush of nerves bubbled up in her tummy like champagne. All of the tales she had told herself this afternoon about Serge Marinov being just some guy disintegrated as she entertained the possibility that she was getting a second chance, and now she could give him one.

Clementine tugged at her dress, straightened her shoulders, and headed over. She wasn't going to make his finding her any more difficult than it needed to be.

There were a lot of people between them, and then there was a break in the crowd and she saw what she had missed before. There was a woman with him—a slender brunette in a sparkly blue dress. She was beautiful, perhaps around thirty, and she had her hand on his arm. It was that territorial display that stopped Clementine in her tracks.

Almost. She'd almost made a fool of herself.

Another woman. Well, that was quick. But what had she expected? Clearly it was exactly what he'd been thinking this morning in that fraught silence. Not, *I'm disappointed Clementine won't be coming with me*. Simply, *Where's the next in line?*

Her shoulders dropped. She felt as if she was getting a crash course in male mating patterns. Was it really that easy for him? She had opened herself up last night to a connection between them and she couldn't close it off so easily. Didn't it mean anything to him?

Clementine stuffed down the sudden sharp pain in her chest. She was such an idiot. Him and Joe Carnegie—both of them deserved flogging. Except, watching Serge now, she recognised he wasn't really anything like Joe. He hadn't hidden anything. He'd been up-front all the way. Probably in his world that was how these things were done. He was hardly going to be her *boyfriend* by any stretch of the imagination. She couldn't imagine him dropping by on a Friday night at her flat with a pizza and lying on the sofa rubbing her feet.

He turned his head suddenly and scanned the crowd, and Clementine froze. She knew when he found her because she felt it like a jolt down to her toes. She recognised the flare of those green eyes, how her own were probably huge in her frozen face. She waited for him to dismiss her, to turn away, but instead his features firmed. He looked resolved.

She spun around before she could see anything that would make mincemeat of her feelings and made her way blindly towards the bar. She needed a drink. She needed hard liquor and fast.

If I'd said yes I could be with him now, she thought helplessly. *I could be in that woman's shoes. I could be going with him to New York.*

She reached the bar and asked for a Bloody Mary. It wasn't

something she normally drank, but she needed something sharp and unfamiliar to snap herself out of this mood. Before it arrived she felt him rather than saw him. The solidity of his body; the turning of other people's heads. There were people everywhere, brushing shoulders, bumping elbows, but she knew it was him.

She gravitated towards him like a planet to the sun and looked up into those eyes of his. She said softly, 'Yes,' then hopelessly, 'I wish I'd said yes. I should have said yes.'

He looked stunned, poleaxed. But at least he didn't look angry or, worse, amused.

I am crazy, thought Clementine. Why did I tell him that? He doesn't care.

Serge experienced the now familiar surge of frustration connected with this woman. What was she playing at?

As Clementine pushed her way through the crowd his first instinct was to pursue her. It was basically his foremost instinct where she was concerned, he acknowledged with more frustration. Yet all he could do was watch her vanish into the crowd, even as his thoughts curled possessively around her admission.

That's the girl. Run away. You won't be getting far.

He had to deal with Raisa before he tried anything bolder with Clementine, and that would take tact, but once he was free he would be going after her.

Clementine had better be able to run fast on those impossible heels of hers, because she'd just declared herself his and he was coming to collect.

CHAPTER FIVE

'Darl, can you cheer up? You're frightening the other passengers.'

'Sorry, I didn't get much shut-eye.' They were queuing to put their bags through at the airport, and at four in the morning she felt just about dead on her feet. But she manufactured a smile for Luke, remembering the old adage to fake it until you make it.

Which she would be applying to her life the minute she got back to London. The last couple of days had impressed on her as nothing else had the need to get back on track with her life. It was time to let the past go. She'd allowed her experience with Joe Carnegie to completely blow anything she might have with Serge Marinov right out of the water. He held a measure of blame, too. If he'd been less forceful she might have been able to navigate around his invitation. Instead they'd both hit a wall—his expectations versus hers—and he had moved on.

'Still thinking about the gorgeous brute?' commented Luke from behind her, resting his chin on her shoulder. 'I thought he was going to pop me one yesterday.'

'I'm sorry about that.' She squeezed his arm. 'I didn't mean for you to get involved.'

'He seems pretty keen on you, Clem.'

'What? No, that's all over.'

'Okey-doke. But I'm not sure he agrees.'

Clementine frowned and moved forward in the queue. Why was Luke speaking in the present tense? Why were people in the queue looking at her?

'Clementine.' His voice turned her around. Deep, dark Russian male.

Serge. So close to her she didn't know where to look. So she looked up and tumbled into his eyes again. It happened each and every time, and she couldn't work out why. Her breath hitched. She didn't know what to say.

His mouth eased into a knowing smile. 'Come with me now to New York, *kisa*.'

Go with him? She was boarding a plane... Of all the unreasonable...

'Are these your bags?'

To her astonishment a young man in a jacket and tie took hold of her suitcase and overnight bag.

'Just a minute—those are my things!'

Serge made a casual gesture with one hand and the guy froze mid-move.

'You have changed your mind?' That smile was still curling wickedly at the corner of his mouth, as if it couldn't possibly be true.

'No, I—' She looked around to find Luke madly nodding at her like a jack-in-the-box.

She rolled her eyes at him.

'Perhaps you would like to say goodbye to your friend and then join me.' Serge's eyes had narrowed on Luke. Clementine already recognised that slight hardening of his mouth.

He was jealous. Well, maybe a teensy weensy bit. Which reminded her...

'What about your girlfriend?'

'*Sto?*' He looked genuinely puzzled.

'Last night. Remember? She was your date. Or are there so many we start to blur?'

Luke snickered.

'Raisa is a friend, nothing more.' He actually sounded a bit affronted, as if he couldn't believe they were having this conversation.

The lady in front of her looked Serge up and down. 'I wouldn't trust him, love. Too good-looking.'

Too good-looking. It was an understatement. He was a big, tough gorgeous Cossack. Every other woman in the vicinity was glued to him.

Clementine bit her lip. It was funny, and she had to admit it was extremely exciting.

She deserved some fun—to be a light-hearted girl again instead of the cautious woman she had become, constantly second-guessing herself.

And he was here. He'd come for her. It was ridiculous to consider any of this romantic but she did. It was the most romantic thing that had ever happened to her.

'All right,' she heard herself saying, throwing herself off the emotional diving board. 'Why not?'

Satisfaction entered the look Serge was giving her, and she noticed a little breathlessly that his gaze took a round trip of her body but she decided to let it pass. Right now she just wanted to revel in her romantic moment.

Serge offered his hand and she took it. It was big and rough and enclosed hers completely. It felt unfailingly intimate. Even this man's hands were fantasy material.

'I'll call you when I arrive,' she said belatedly to Luke, who was grinning and gazing up at Serge like a fan girl.

'You do that, Clem. Have fun, darl.'

They had only gone a few hundred metres when she realised they were moving away from the public terminal.

'Where are we going?'

'My plane, *kisa*.'

'Your plane?'

'Private jet.' He glanced down at her and was met with a look of complete wonderment. Cynically, he wondered if that little bit of information was going to get him laid before the plane even took off.

She dug in her heels as they left the terminal and hit the tarmac. Ahead was indeed a private plane—a state-of-the-art jet. Nerves set in like never before. She yanked on his hand. 'Serge, I need to make a few things clear before we go any further.'

He looked at her impatiently. 'We'll discuss it on board.'

'No, we need to discuss it now. I have...' She didn't know how to phrase it, so she grabbed the nearest equivalent. 'I have some terms and I want to make sure you're okay with them. I don't want any misunderstandings.'

He gave her a look of sheer disbelief. 'You cannot be serious?'

Her heart stuttered at that. He wasn't going to be difficult about this, was he? It wasn't a deal-breaker?

'I am serious,' she said more crossly. 'And I want to be up-front about this.' She'd come to a complete halt, pulling free of his hand. 'I don't want to be treated like some girl you've just picked up.'

He made a sound of deep male frustration in the back of his throat. 'I have no intention of treating you as anything but a lady. Frankly, Clementine, in Russia we do not do things in this way. Would you not prefer some discretion?'

Baffled she gazed up at him. He would treat her *as* a lady? Why didn't that reassure her? Shouldn't he *consider* her a lady?

Suddenly it all felt too hard, and she decided then and there to let it go. She was reading too much into everything he said because she was having trouble trusting anyone. It wasn't fair to Serge, and it was going to ruin things before they started.

'We can discuss your terms when we're alone, *kisa*,' he said dryly. 'But I can assure you there won't be any "misunderstandings" as you describe it.'

She laid her hand gently on his chest. He felt so hard, and she could feel the shift of muscle as he took a deep breath. She affected him, and it thrilled her because it answered her own desire for him. But it wasn't anything she was going to act on unless it felt absolutely right.

She smiled up at him—her first for the day. 'I'm really glad you came for me, Serge.'

'You like the jet, *kisa*?'

'I guess.' She gave a gasp as he slid his arm around her waist and scooped her up into his arms.

'Serge!'

'*Da*—Serge.'

The sudden physical closeness wrapped around her and she melted. That fast she was a mess of hormones and longing.

He carried her as if she weighed nothing. Something long dormant inside her leapt in answer to his overt masculine display of physical strength and dominance. He was taking her over, and it was stunningly clear her body liked it.

Serge experienced a primitive satisfaction in having Clementine in his arms. He'd been anticipating this since last night. He'd been working towards it since he'd followed her down the Nevsky. Elusive Clementine, who withheld so much, only made him want more, to give her more.

Those terms of hers… Never had he been confronted with such a bald request from a woman. Did she imagine he wasn't going to cough up with the gifts? And how high exactly did she measure her favours? Not that it really mattered; at this point he was prepared to pay any price.

* * *

'How much does all this cost?'

Clementine ground to a halt in her silver slingbacks and did a three-sixty as she took in the hotel foyer. Understated elegance had never looked so expensive. Adding it to the limo from JFK, the posse of minders following them in another car, and not forgetting the plane—the private jet—the world was starting to resemble Oz, of the Wizard variety.

Serge waited, dark green eyes steady on her, his hand extended in a gesture to have her join him.

'Okay, Slugger—spill.' She sashayed up to him and slid her hand into his as if she accompanied wealthy, powerful men into hotels every day of the week.

'This sports management gig—who in heck do you manage?'

'Not who, *kisa*, what.' His expression was indulgent, as if she entertained him. 'I own a corporation that broadcasts and hosts boxing and mixed martial arts fights.'

Clementine batted her eyelashes at him. 'Wow,' she said. 'That's—wow.'

'I'm getting an impressed vibe from you, Clementine.'

The entire twelve hours of the flight—half of which she had slept—Serge had been an exemplary host, seeing to her needs before retreating behind his laptop and work. But she was definitely getting a more playful Serge now that they were on *terra firma*.

He ushered her into the elevator and the doors closed out the rest of the world. Serge's shoulders rose up in front of her and Clementine couldn't see anything else but him.

'Where I come from your line of business translates as very blokey. It explains a lot.'

And there it was—that little private smile he'd been waiting for.

He gently twined her hair over her shoulder and said quietly, close to her ear, 'And what does it explain, Clementine?'

She shivered in response. 'All the testosterone. That's why you were able to beat off those guys. You knew what you were doing.' Her own voice had grown hushed. She looked up at him.

'Since meeting you, *kisa*, it's been the only thing I've been sure of doing.' His admission, meant only to tease her, suddenly hit him as absolute fact.

She batted those lashes more slowly. 'You're not sure of me, Slugger?'

'Clementine, I have a feeling no man has ever been sure of you.'

His hand moved around her waist. He leaned in and gave her a moment to accept he was going to kiss her, and then his mouth was suddenly hot and moving fast against her own, opening her up with his tongue, tasting her, giving her no time to back away.

He hauled her up against him and Clementine turned to liquid heat. She moaned helplessly and slid her arms up around his neck, powerless against the feelings he was stoking in her. His body felt so hard against her own, and the slide of his tongue over her lower lip found an answering pulse deep down inside her. It was almost too much.

The doors slid open with a soft ping and Serge broke their kiss. It had only lasted a matter of moments, but it felt like for ever, and Clementine couldn't believe she'd got so carried away from one kiss. Mouth trembling, nipples pressing tight and hot against the lace of her bra, she pulled at her dress. The silk jersey had risen up over her thighs and her hair felt tangled and messy from his hands.

She watched him use a keycard on the door, trying to clear her head. She hadn't known a kiss could undo her, and suddenly all her certainty about what she was doing began to fall away.

Serge ushered her inside, his hand on the small of her back.

She needed to keep a clear head if she was going to navigate these waters. 'Wow,' she said inadequately as she stepped into sheer luxury. 'This is—incredible.'

The extravagance of the hotel suite was another reminder of exactly who Serge was. A rich man. Who could buy a great deal to keep himself happy. No doubt including women.

But not this woman. She needed to make that very clear to him. Somehow.

'I'm not that impressed, you know, Slugger. Money doesn't do it for me.'

'What *does* do it for you, Clementine?' He was smiling at her, that big, lazy Russian male smile, as if he knew something she didn't.

'Honesty,' she replied. 'Sincerity.'

The smile darkened to something else. She'd surprised him.

Her pulse was going thumpity-thumpity as she made her way slowly through the rooms—the living area, the dining room with seating for twenty-four, past the baby grand. She stopped to run her fingers down an octave.

'You play, *kisa*?'

'By ear.' She lifted her gaze to his heated expression and a rush of sweet arousal washed through her body. 'I'm a quick study.'

She backed away from the piano, realised Serge was measuring her with his gaze. She needed to keep her wits about her with this man. She needed to keep up the banter, hold him off a little longer until she got herself back under control. Beckoning to him with one manicured finger, she fashioned a smile. 'Come on, Slugger, we'll see what else we can find.'

Her heart was pounding as she strolled into the bedroom, knowing her big Siberian tiger was following.

Cheeks pink, breathing shallow, she put her head in at the *en suite* bathroom door.

'Now, that is one big tub.'

'Would you like to make use of it, Clementine?' he said from behind her.

'Not right now.' She was astonished at how steady her voice was.

She felt his body only centimetres from her own, and she tensed. She had to be smart about this.

She heard her zip start to slide down and suddenly knew she couldn't do it. It came over her in a panic, most unlike her, and she pulled away.

A few days ago she'd wondered if she could handle him. She was fast discovering her answer was no. A resounding no.

Jerking around, she put a hand up as if she were stopping traffic. 'Hang on a minute, Slugger, we've only just got here.' Her voice sounded ridiculously girlish. 'How about dinner and a movie first?'

She could feel the heat coming off his body, the slam of his breathing as his chest rose and fell just inches from hers. He slid one big hand around her waist, pulling her towards him, smiling that wicked smile of his, and she realised he wasn't taking her seriously at all.

'Hey.' She shoved at his chest with one hand and pulled on his arm with the other. 'I'm not playing, mister. Hands to yourself.'

She couldn't be serious? He frowned. By all that was holy, she *was* serious. Serge released her slowly, but Clementine backed up so fast she hit the doorframe of the *en suite* bathroom, banging her head.

Bringing up her hand to rub the offended spot, she blinked at him warily. 'I said dinner and a movie,' she repeated mulishly, not liking feeling this way—a little foolish and on the back foot.

She kept her eyes on his, daring him to argue her down.

She wasn't a newbie at this, but Serge Marinov was something beyond her experience. She just didn't feel ready to be that out of control, and that kiss in the lift had rung some pretty significant bells. This man could very well annihilate all her inhibitions, and she really, really didn't want to wake up tomorrow morning to a note on the pillow telling her thanks, he'd be in touch.

She wasn't naive. She got the impression Serge saw her as a lot more sophisticated than she actually was, and she probably needed to talk to him about that. Which made dinner an excellent idea.

'Dinner and a movie?' he echoed. 'They're your terms, *kisa*?'

Clementine wanted to flap her lashes and tell him yes, but she'd been shaken up by what had just happened and it wasn't fair to Serge to keep up the flirting when she so clearly wasn't going to follow through.

'Not terms. I just thought it would be nice,' she offered. 'Normal.'

Nice. Normal. Serge was trying to get his head around what had just happened. One minute he was being lured by a siren into the bedroom, and the next he was shipwrecked on the rocks—an uncouth oaf who had come on too strong and not taken no for an answer.

He was thrown back to that café in Petersburg, feeling like a thug for upsetting Clementine. She was either playing a very clever game or he had got this all very wrong. If he had it wrong, and this less than sure of herself Clementine who kept appearing at inopportune times was the real deal, the traditional Russian male that lurked not far below his modern sensibility was going to have a field-day. And he needed to keep that firmly in check.

He knew which way that led.

Either way, he wouldn't rush her. It would do both of them

a disservice. Especially if what was between them turned out to be as incendiary as he suspected it would.

Clementine decanted her clothes into one of the guest bedrooms, wondering what on earth she thought she was doing. Serge had got changed and told her he was going down to use the gym for a couple of hours. He would return to take her to dinner at seven.

She had hoped to spend a little time in his company beforehand, but given her actions this afternoon she hadn't felt in a position to try and dissuade him. He'd said something about having some excess energy to work off, which she might have interpreted as flattering. Instead it had just fallen flat.

Folding the last of her T-shirts away, she plopped down on the guest bed and smoothed one hand over the gold satin quilt. She was definitely in luxury land, with a man she didn't know nearly enough about, but there was a huge part of her that was singing out *squeee* as she threw herself down the rocky, rushing ravine she just knew this week with Serge would be. He'd almost pulled her over into the rapids with him this afternoon, but she'd balked at the last minute.

Cautious Clementine. She grimaced at Luke's nickname for her and checked her watch. Serge had been gone barely an hour. Smiling to herself, she began peeling off her clothes.

Serge repetitively drummed the gloves into the bag, feeling the shudder through his arms, relishing the impact. He couldn't believe the scene he'd had with Clementine. It took him back to being seventeen and not sure if it was all right to put his hand under a girl's top if she hadn't explicitly given permission.

Sweat blinded him and he pulled the punches, stepped away from the bag and reached for a towel, rubbing his face.

As he slung it over his shoulder he reached for his bottle of water.

'Is this what you're looking for?' Clementine stood in front of him, offering up the bottle with a little smile.

She was wearing a tiny pair of red shorts and a white tank top, and she'd tied all that hair back in a ponytail.

'Thanks,' he said, almost by rote, as every male cell in his body sat up and saluted.

'Can I have a go?' She indicated the punching bag.

'It might be a bit hard for you,' he responded, trying not to ogle her. Something Clementine was clearly aware of, judging by the little smile she was wearing.

His knowing, provocative little Clementine was back.

'Just give me some gloves, Slugger.'

He fetched a smaller pair for her hands and attached them himself, watching her expression as she tried not to stroke his body too obviously with her gaze. The urge to haul her against him and take what he wanted was very strong. 'Go in close,' he instructed. 'Little jabs. Keep your elbows up. That's it—don't pull back.'

Her concentration was absolute. She was really taking this seriously. His gaze dropped momentarily to the superlative curve of her bottom in those little shorts. Had she purposely come down here to shred the last fibres of his self-control?

She gave an *oomph* as the bag swung back and knocked her onto that bottom. She lay back laughing on the mat, looking up at him towering over her. As she watched he stripped off the sweat-soaked T-shirt he was wearing and stood there in only a pair of baggy long shorts that were barely holding onto his lean hips. There was something else stirring that made Clementine's laughter trickle into a deep sigh of feminine satisfaction. His shoulders and chest and back were powerful and heavily muscled, and there was a haze of dark hair arrowing down below his navel she longed to run her hands through. But after her little performance earlier in the day she didn't feel entitled.

He offered her a hand and she took it. One-armed, he literally pulled her off the ground and to her feet. As a display of strength it was breathtaking. But what really took her breath away was standing up so close to his barely clothed body, with her own hardly left to the imagination. He ran those green eyes over her face and then lower, to where her nipples were very clearly making themselves known.

'Are we really waiting until after dinner and the movie, *dushka*?'

His voice ran over her like rough velvet.

She licked her lips. No was on the tip of her tongue when other voices interrupted and Serge turned away, cursing under his breath.

'A public gym,' murmured Clementine. 'Whoops.'

Three men had come through the doors at the other end of the weights room.

'I'll hit the shower,' said Serge. 'You go on up. But keep the little outfit on.'

She narrowed her eyes and gave him a push to one rock-hard bicep. 'Dinner, Slugger. But I'll give you a raincheck for the movie.'

Clementine was surprised when Serge insisted on walking her out before returning to change and shower. He really was an old-fashioned guy in so many respects, and that was playing nicely with her inner princess. He wasn't just muscles and testosterone; he had some stellar qualities—manners being one of them.

She showered herself, and put on a red and gold kaftan dress that wrapped around and tied at the waist. It was simple, but she could dress it up with heeled sandals and she swept her hair up, attaching a red silk flower behind her ear.

She layered on the kohl and the false eyelashes and painted her lips ruby-red.

She heard Serge's sports bag drop and scooted out to meet him. He took one look at her outfit and put up his hands. 'I surrender, Clementine. Dinner.'

She grinned.

CHAPTER SIX

THEY dined not in the hotel but at an exclusive restaurant on Manhattan's Upper East Side. The menu was contemporary French cuisine, but frankly, Clementine thought, she could have been eating sushi and she wouldn't have noticed.

The man opposite her in a suit and tie, all elegant Manhattan urbanity, fixated all of her attention. He hadn't rushed her off to bed, he hadn't pushed anything, and now he was dining with her in the most civilised surroundings imaginable. Their conversation ranged over her life in London, his here in New York, current events. But every time she allowed her gaze to settle on him—whether it be the breadth of his naked wrist beneath the fabric of his sleeve, the wide column of his strong neck so snugly contained in a collar and tie, the faint cleft in his chin that she imagined was tricky to shave— she kept picturing him standing over her, half-naked, dripping sweat and testosterone in that gym. Exactly as she had fantasised about him the first moment she'd clapped eyes on him.

Warmth pooled low in her pelvis and had been there for much of their meal. The wine and the soup and the main course and a blackberry dessert had all slid down, and her cheeks grew pink and her eyes sparkled as she listened to the deep, rhythmically accented voice stroking her senses, watching the changing colours in his sea-green eyes like the tides. She knew she had made the right decision in coming to New York with him.

No more cold showers, thought Serge as he helped Clementine out of the cab. His libido stretched and did a few push-ups in readiness.

They could have taken a town car, but she had wanted the 'fun' of riding in a New York City taxi cab—and who was he to spoil Clementine's fun?

Half of the sheer enjoyment he was having with her was watching her reactions to little things. She had the most expressive face he had ever seen, and it was because of that he knew her skittishness earlier had not been part of some ploy to stoke his desire for her or even some odd kink of her own. She genuinely hadn't been ready. But she was ready now— or his reading of female arousal was completely off-kilter.

Given the woman he was with, that was always possible.

So they were back to square one as the lift flew them skywards to the fifty-third floor, but he didn't attempt to touch her. He wanted to be very sure Clementine was on board with the programme. He also wanted to discuss a few terms of his own. He didn't want there to be any 'misunderstandings' when this was all over—and it would be over at some point. But thinking about the end before they even really began pulled him up short.

With another woman he would have discussed this long ago, but with Clementine he had delayed. Now there was a certain necessity in the moment to rush her into bed and to hell with everything else.

He hesitated to call it romanticism, but Clementine had early on introduced a certain element of that into their situation—he wouldn't call it a relationship—when she'd made herself so elusive in St Petersburg. He wanted to do this right. He wanted to do it the old-fashioned way and sweep her off her feet.

Which he did—after opening the door, gathering her into his arms and enjoying her gasp of surprise. Women loved to be carried, and Clementine was no exception to the rule. She wrapped her strong slender arms around his neck, her soft hair tickling his chin. What was different was how good it felt holding her this way. It probably had something to do with her elusiveness again. She couldn't run off, and all the muscles in her body seemed to dissolve as she submitted to his superior strength.

He'd never thought of himself as the sort of man who got off on proving himself to women, but her reaction to him lifting her off the floor this afternoon—a spontaneous gesture—and again being carried now was doing a power of good to his ego. Which boded well for tonight.

The lights in the suite were sensor-activated, and they showered across them as he carried her into the living area and she wriggled out of his arms. His intention was to take her off guard by kissing her and letting things run from there. And judging by his hardening body they'd be running pretty fast.

'Let's make some coffee and a little chat,' she suggested, tugging on his hand and taking a few backward steps, intending to pull him with her.

'Let's not.' He hauled her back in with one hand and she looked up at him, faint apprehension behind those steady grey eyes. Then her lashes dipped down and she seemed to make up her mind.

Slowly, cautiously, she reached up and wound her arms around his neck. But before she could press those soft lips to his he reached down and made short work of the bow at her waist, letting her go only to unravel the fabric that tied her kaftan together. He'd been studying that bow all night, in preparation for this moment, and the effect was well worth it as Clementine gave a shocked little yelp.

But she didn't try to cover herself, and when he began pulling the dress gently down off her shoulders she wriggled to give it a hand, pressing up against him in nothing but her sheer black bra and knickers. He fancied she was trying to shield herself. He felt rather than saw her step out of her heels.

She suddenly felt much smaller and somehow less assured in his arms. The dress slid down at his third tug and pooled on the floor. He ran his hand along her spine, coming to rest on the curve of her delectable bottom.

'I'm feeling a bit naked here, Slugger,' she said, but it was the nervous laugh that took him off guard. He hadn't expected her to be uncertain. 'Can't we do this in the bedroom, like normal people?'

'What is this "normal" you keep talking about?' he teased, his voice heavy with his arousal. 'This feels normal to me, *kisa*.'

'Not all of us normally swing from chandeliers,' she prevaricated, but he noticed she began pushing his jacket over his shoulders, and he helped her. Then she was pulling at his shirt-tails, but he wanted to see her face.

He tucked a finger under her chin, drew her eyes up to his. 'I promise no chandelier-swinging—even if you beg.'

Her grey eyes grew unbelievably soft, her whole expressive face somehow radiating a warmth and trust he knew he didn't deserve. For a moment he was distracted with the thought that the woman in his arms was taking all of this far too seriously for his comfort.

But his blood was pumping, and if he didn't learn every inch of her body tonight he was going to explode.

Clementine made his decision as she reached up and wound her arms around his neck. He gave way to the rush of desire he had to possess her, to know her.

Clementine heard him murmur something in Russian and his hands spread over her hips, moving down to cup her bottom as he drew her up to kiss her. His mouth was everything she remembered, hot, but tender this time, stealing her breath and any free will she had left. He seduced her with his mouth, kissing her mindless, until it was his body, hard and muscular, she began to explore helplessly.

She reached for the button and zip on his trousers, slipping her hand inside. She gave a little murmur of surprise. She gently learned his size and shape as he breathed heavily, his chest rising and falling with flattering intensity.

'Keep that up, *kisa,* and this may be over before we know it,' he murmured, his voice deep and dark in her ear.

'I don't believe that,' she whispered back, but he scooped her up and finally carried her through the other rooms and into the bedroom, lying her down on the slippery white satin quilting. Then methodically he began to unbutton his shirt.

Clementine lay back, biting her lip as she watched his big shoulders emerge and then his chest, broad and heavy with muscle, hazy with the dark hair she remembered, his powerful arms next, his waist, lean and defined.

Then he shucked off his trousers and boxers and long, muscular hair-roughened thighs and calves came into view, and what she'd had her hand on only minutes before. And then he came down onto the bed with her.

His hand cupped her face and he turned her mouth towards his before his lips brushed over hers, and then he was kissing her slowly, sensuously, dragging his fingers through her hair, loosing it so that it toppled down, a heavy mass that swam across his shoulder and bicep as he supported her.

His big rough hand curled into the underside of her left knee, stroked her there, moved up under the length of her thigh to squeeze the lush curve of her bottom.

Clementine trembled as his fingers pushed up the delicate silk of her knickers, anticipating every move he was making. But when his hand continued its exploration over her hip, dipping into her waist and smoothing up over her ribs, covering her breast encased in the same silk of her knickers, it wasn't familiar. He wasn't going for broke. He was taking his time.

His thumb made a slow perambulation of her nipple and his mouth caught hers again in a slow, sweet kiss as he gently handled her body.

'I knew you would have an amazing body,' he told her appreciatively, 'and it's more beautiful than I imagined.'

She reached behind and unhooked her bra for him, baring her breasts and trying not to show the faint ripple of anxiety she was feeling.

'It just gets better,' he murmured, that flaring gaze sweeping over her. He framed one breast with his hand, exploring the shape of her, bending his head to take her nipple into his mouth.

Clementine made a helpless noise and arched her back, the rhythms of her body taking over. She knew how to do this, or thought she did, but Serge seemed to know her body better than she did.

When she was almost crying with need and distraction he lifted his head, only to abrade her nipple lightly with the bristly skin along his jaw, watching her shudder. It had never been like this for her before—the want, the magic of having one hundred per cent of a man's attention on her pleasure. This man's attention—knowing, practised, skilled—was beyond her experience.

His hand slid down over her hip and he hooked a thumb under her knickers, and then he was sliding down the bed, settling between her thighs, and with a wink he applied his mouth to the heart of her.

Clementine threw back her head and whimpered as little starbursts of sensation blurred her vision. She felt swollen and ultra-sensitive, and when his tongue swiped over her clitoris she went with it, her cries filling the warmly lit room.

Serge shifted up over her, pausing only briefly to don a condom. Then suddenly he was inside her. He only gave her a moment to adjust before he was moving, and the sensations began to build again. She found her own body matching his rhythm. She clasped him around the neck and he forged his mouth to hers in deep open-mouthed kisses that mingled their breath and tongues with Russian words Clementine didn't understand but knew had to do with how good this was. His eyes were dark with pleasure and he kept making eye contact with her, as if testing the depth of her enjoyment but also letting her see his.

She could hear his deep rasping breathing, the heavy thump of his heartbeat, smell the warm musky scent of his male skin. A light sheen of sweat had broken on the broad expanse of his back and she luxuriated in that too, loving the intense maleness of him. Then it happened. An unexpected series of sweet, unending undulations crashed through her pelvis, spreading all the way out to her fingers and her toes, making the hair on her head stand up.

'Serge!'

'*Da*—Serge.' In response he thrust harder and faster.

Her orgasm met her and she rolled with it. She was contracting around him, and with a deep groan he released into her. It went on and on, spiralling through her body as she unravelled. As he subsided she sank back into the mattress, taking him heavily down on top of her, loving the sensation of being utterly consumed by him.

She closed her eyes and breathed him in. Her Cossack.

Clementine felt the absence of his weight even though he had only lain heavily atop her so briefly. He had his eyes closed and gave a couple of deep, gusty breaths, as if bringing himself back to reality. She knew how he felt. She hardly recognised herself in the woman who had clung to him and whimpered, encouraging him to do more, to make her feel more.

She turned her head on the pillow and looked at him.

Beautiful. He'd called her beautiful.

She gathered the word up close and hugged it. She felt beautiful.

She reached out and touched his shoulder. His head tilted and his green gaze tangled with hers. Her heart gave a sudden lovely thump and her pulse kicked up.

Serge rolled towards her and brushed his thumb back and forth over her cheek, traced her mouth. 'I thought I'd dreamed you up in that store,' he said in a gravelly voice, 'but here you are. All mine.'

Clementine's eyes went soft as down even as Serge's own thoughts raced to a stunning halt. He didn't know what it was he wanted from her, but it wasn't this. Closeness…connection. What in the hell had prompted his soft words?

'Serge, make love to me,' she invited, lashes lowering, mouth soft, her body recumbent beneath him, parting her thighs in explicit invitation. She was a fantasy he had never known he had. Until now.

This at least he understood. This he could do. Again and again.

'My pleasure,' he said, and moved over her.

She drifted to consciousness to find herself alone. For a moment Clementine wondered if it had all been an erotic dream, before she rolled over into the space where he had slept and buried her face in his pillow, seeking out the remnants of his scent. No dream. All real. Luckiest girl in the world.

There was a tender ache between her thighs. In fact all of her was a bit achy. Memories assailed her—his hands on her, those skilful hands. A big smile spread over her face. Where had he learned to do those things? Had she really let him? When would they do it again? She sat up and winced. Maybe not this morning.

Should she get up and go and find him? What was she going to say? Maybe he wasn't a morning person. She definitely wasn't—with the exception of this morning. Sinking back onto his side of the bed, she luxuriated in her happy place. Nothing could ruin this feeling.

Stretching, she felt her hand land on something hard and cold beside the pillow. Curiously she rolled over, put her hand on a small red box.

Even as she opened it a chill was spreading through her chest.

Diamonds glittered from a black velvet bed. She couldn't even bring herself to touch them. There was a note attached.

Wear this tonight. I'll be back for you at seven. Dress up.

Clementine didn't know how long she sat there, crosslegged in the bed, the jewellery case abandoned beside her, the note shouting at her: *He's bought you; he thinks you're for sale.*

It took a while for the storm of feeling inside her to subside, but it did, and then she began to think more rationally.

Serge had no idea about her past. He couldn't know a piece of jewellery like this would push her buttons. Sensibly she told herself this was probably his *modus operandi*. Get the girl, drape her in something glittery—the same way other men bought flowers.

Oh, flowers would have been nice—to wake up to a little bunch of something beside her. Would have cost him a great deal less, too.

She wilted a little and gave a wry smile.

Serge Marinov might be a rich guy who flew in women to warm his bed, but that wasn't all he was. She'd seen enough to know this was a really good guy. She would never have slept with him last night if he wasn't.

He had been everything—tender and passionate and romantic.

He just didn't have a clue about the morning after.

She picked up the jewellery case and shoved it into the bedside table, then padded barefoot out of the bedroom. Out of sight, out of mind.

All morning long he'd been thinking about her. Through a tedious meeting with the stadium committee, a photo opportunity downtown at the Mayor's office, putting in a bid on some venues in California, his thoughts had continuously returned to the sleeping girl he had left at dawn.

Several times he'd almost rung her cell, self-preservation muscling in each time. The minute he phoned her he would be opening up a channel of communication between his working life and the woman in his bed. He'd never done it before. He wasn't starting now.

'Serge, you're not with us,' Mick's voice intervened, dragging him back into the present and his office in Upper Manhattan.

No, he wasn't with them. Serge corralled his stampeding thoughts about a six-foot girl naked in his bed and looked at the stats Alex had handed him. Mick's word was good enough, but Alex Khardovsky, president of the Marinov Corporation, always came up with cold hard numbers, and Serge knew at the end of the day you could trust figures. Unlike people, they never let you down.

'So you'll come down and have a look at the kid?' Mick was saying.

Dinner with Clementine. He was going to have to postpone it.

'I'll meet you there at seven.' He'd divert on his way across town and drop in at the hotel—enjoy a quickie with the beautiful girl he had left in his bed.

'I want to go over these figures with you, Serge. Can we grab a bite and meet Mick at the gym?'

'No, I need to drop in at the hotel. I'll take these with me.'

Alex grinned. 'A woman? I thought you seemed unusually upbeat.'

Usually Serge wouldn't have hesitated to affirm or deny a question from Alex. He was his oldest friend. They had been in boot camp together. Apart from Mick he was the only other person he trusted. Happily married for three years, Alex joked that the only excitement he got these days was observing Serge's revolving door policy on women.

But the memory of Clementine's soft grey eyes as he cuddled her close struck him as he opened his mouth, and he closed it. Shook his head briefly.

'We still need to talk about Kolcek,' said Mick flatly. 'You have to do more than a press conference, son. You need to put your face to the brand.'

Serge folded his arms. 'And I'm the poster boy for good clean living?'

Alex snorted, but Mick shook his head. 'Publicity's everything in this game, and you both know it. Your image is hardly what the moms at home are applauding, and that's what this political stunt over Kolcek is aimed at. The punters like to see you with a different airhead every day in the papers, but not the general public. You need to be seen with a decent woman at your side. Geez, I shouldn't have to tell you boys this.'

'I'm not playing the media game, Mick,' stated Serge with finality. 'The business is one thing, my private life another.'

'The problem being there's nothing private about it. What about that woman who spilled her guts about "my life with fight promoter Serge Marinov—the highs and lows of a jet-set playboy"?' Mick threw the magazine he'd been carrying around onto the desk between them.

Serge ignored it. 'I barely knew the woman—slept with her twice. Once too many.'

Alex picked up the magazine. 'I'll show this to Abbey. She'll love it.'

Serge smiled, seeing the lighter side of it. Alex's wife took him to task about his lifestyle every time their paths crossed.

It wasn't until Mick and Alex were gone that he was given the opportunity to phone Clementine's cell. She gave him that breathless 'Serge' he was beginning to look forward to, and promised to be at the hotel in half an hour.

It was on the tip of his tongue to ask if she'd had a good day, but he knew the minute he did that he'd be feeding into a fantasy that she was in his life in any other way than his bed. His mind went back to the trashy magazine and the brunette he barely remembered. She'd sold her story for five figures, he'd heard. He couldn't quite picture Clementine selling anything.

He'd been right not to mention her name to Alex.

'See you then.' Her voice was in his ear, and was he just feeling extremely restless or did he hear a note of longing? Grinning, he rang off.

The penthouse was quiet as Clementine let herself in, but all the lights were on. She was sticky from her long day sightseeing, and wanted to bathe and get changed, but her heart had started paddling like a kayak up a canyon the closer she'd got to the hotel, knowing Serge would be inside waiting for her.

The intimacy they had built up, culminating in last night, felt a million miles away. Not being with him today, in the aftermath of their incredible night, had left her emotions close to the surface and she was feeling a little nervous—but also excited.

He was standing out on the balcony, those muscular arms of his spread on the railing, supporting him as he looked out over the city. From behind he was all masculine grace, with his lean height and the powerful spread of his shoulders. Clementine experienced an inner trembling as her body recognised what it liked. She'd never known anything like it when she was with him. It was as if the air between them lit up like sheet lightning.

She stopped on the threshold of the balcony. 'Hi,' she said, endeavouring to sound as casual as she could.

He turned around, and the intensity of his gaze was full of everything they had shared. The answering pulse in her body brought soft colour to her cheeks.

'Hi yourself,' he answered, as if he knew what was happening to her.

'Busy day?' She knew she sounded inane, but her heart was pounding.

'They're all busy, *kisa*.' He smiled slowly. 'You're late.' But it was said without animosity.

'Am I?' She knew she was. But he hadn't been beside her when she woke up. So let him deal with it, niggled the thought, and a little of her excitement fluttered away.

He strolled inside, shutting the glass doors on the city behind him, and casually reached for her. As his big hands slid over her hips, bringing her up against him, she experienced a flare of longing in her body that had nothing to do with the resistance in her head.

She waited for him to say something, allude in some way to this morning, but he merely bent his head and kissed her.

Clementine put her hands up to his chest and gently disengaged herself with a murmured, 'Not so fast.'

He released her, disconcerting her by patting her on the backside. 'Off you go, then.'

She looked at him uncertainly. 'I'll just go and change. I

won't be more than twenty minutes.' She hesitated, feeling a little shy all of a sudden. 'Are we going somewhere fancy?'

'There's been a change of plan.' He turned his back on her as he strolled over to the side table to collect his phone and keys. 'I've got to go downtown tonight. I can't take you out to dinner.'

'You're going out?'

'It's work, Clementine. Happens all the time.' His expression said *get used to it.*

'That's okay,' she replied, determinedly cheerful. 'I'll come with you.'

'You'll come—' He broke off, frowning at her. 'No, it's not a place for you.'

Her hand found her hip. 'What is it? A mosque?'

'A gym,' he said briefly. 'A lot of sweat and testosterone.'

'So a lot like last night?' she replied, scooting after him as he headed over to the wet bar.

He slowed to a halt, turned. Some of the tension eased around his mouth. He smiled. 'Maybe, but without the important addition of a soft landing.'

It was the smile that got to her. She narrowed her eyes. 'Did you just describe me as a soft landing?'

'You supplied the soft landing, Clementine. I would describe *you* as a miracle of natural engineering.'

Somehow it wasn't a compliment. It wasn't what you said to the woman you'd made love to for the first time and then abandoned the next morning. *Yes, Clementine*, a little voice niggled. Abandoned.

She didn't like the way he catalogued her body either—as if examining the parts he liked best. Guys did that to her a lot. It made her feel less than a person. She wanted him to see the whole woman—had imagined he had last night. But she guessed that wasn't the reality.

Unimpressed, she muttered, 'Careful with the sweet-talk, Slugger, you'll melt my knickers off.'

He grinned. He liked her like this—making him work for it. The other Clementine—softer, a little unsure of herself—put the wrong thoughts in his head. Thoughts of looking after her.

This Clementine could look after herself.

He relaxed.

'I'm going to freshen up,' she said stiltedly, a little afraid that when she came back he would be gone. 'It's been a long day.'

Serge didn't attempt to stop her. She had a right to be annoyed with him. He wasn't going to be able to do justice to her beautiful body this week with so much going on in the outside world. But he could make it up to her now—soothe that little temper of hers in a mutually satisfactory way.

Clementine satisfied herself by calling him every name in the book as she stripped off in the bathroom, stepping into the pressure-activated shower and letting the warm water do its soothing job. Where was the sweet, attentive man who'd listened to her over dinner and held her hand going in and out of the restaurant, who'd been so romantic with her last night?

Gone the way of the fairies, Clementine. Because he never existed. Now that he'd had her he'd cooled off. She'd heard about guys like him. Once the chase was over so was the romance. She snorted. She'd been such an idiot. The romance she'd been hoping for hadn't even got off the ground because there never *had* been any romance.

Serge knocked once, for appearances' sake, then opened the bathroom door. There she was—one of his afternoon's fantasies come to life. All six feet of naked Clementine, with water running over her pale honey skin, the graceful seashell-pink-tipped breasts, the narrow waist that only made the extravagant flare of her hips and bottom all the more dramatic, and those long, long legs.

She turned, sensing him, and those lovely eyes of hers narrowed.

'Don't even try it, Marinov.'

But he knew the battles he could win, and this was one of them.

Fully dressed, he stepped under the water stream, hands sliding around her. When she opened her mouth to swear a blue streak at him he took it as his invitation to lower his head and kiss her.

Clementine put up a good fight against her desire for him, holding off for at least five seconds before she spread her hands over his shoulders and pressed herself up against him. With his arms around her he felt solid and exciting, and everything fell away except for this. The way he made her feel. Beautiful, wanted, safe.

So many firsts, she thought later as she sat on the bed, wrapped in a big warm towel, knowing she needed to go and get dressed.

It was all playing through her head. Serge hadn't even removed his clothes—just unzipped and it had been happening, and her need had climbed with his at breakneck speed. What was wrong with her? She should have yelled at him—not had sex with him.

He was treating her like a convenience.

It was never more obvious than when he came out of the *en suite* bathroom, towelling dry his hair. He glanced at the digital clock and swore softly in Russian.

More disappointed with him by the minute, she said sharply, 'Going to be late, Serge? Never mind—just tell your friends you couldn't keep it zipped up. I'm sure it's not the first time.'

He dropped the towel to his side. He looked genuinely shocked.

Good. For five whole seconds she had a little payback.

But then he drawled, 'It's work, Clementine, and it's twenty-four-seven. Welcome to my world.' He threw the towel onto a chair and slid open a drawer. 'And, by the way, crudity doesn't suit you. I'd prefer you continued to behave like the lady you are.'

'Except when I've got my legs wrapped around your waist in the shower,' she shot back, hurt.

He flashed a charismatic smile over his shoulder. 'Exactly.'

Oh, boy. A streak of healthy cleansing anger ripped through her body. She was *so* out of here. His week of pleasure had just got foreshortened to one night. When he got back she'd be gone. Over the hills. Far, far away.

But even as she formed the thought of escape she dug her toes a little more firmly into the carpet. Oh, yes, Clementine, look at you running. Like *that's* going to happen. You've never been with a man like this and it's exciting, and despite everything you want to at least try and see if this can go somewhere better. Besides, he's got you wrapped around his little finger and he knows it. Why would he let you go yet? As long as he wants you you'll stay.

And with that all the anger fell away and all she felt was confusion.

What was going on? Was she sulking? Serge tugged on some briefs, pulled on his jeans. Glanced over at her again.

She was snapping at him as if he'd done something to disappoint her. Yet she'd climaxed around him in the shower. Hadn't she?

Was that the problem? Had she been faking it? The thought brought him up cold. He prided himself on giving a woman the pleasure she deserved in exchange for the gift of her body, and the notion that he hadn't lived up to Clementine's expectations wiped out any thought other than remedying that.

He strolled over and dropped to his knees at her feet. Clementine stared at him in astonishment as he tugged playfully on her towel, parting it to reveal her thighs.

'What are you doing?'

'Makings things better. Lie back, *kisa*, and think happy thoughts.'

He had to be joking. Clementine grabbed the towel and pulled it back down to her knees, tucking her legs up under her as fast as she could. 'Don't you dare.'

A challenge? A wicked smile lit up his face, but no answering invitation came from Clementine.

She glared at him. 'Your bedside manner needs a lot of work, mate.'

The smile was gone. In its place was disbelief. 'You love it, *kisa*.'

The sheer arrogance of the man! 'Love what? Being pawed at?' Her voice trembled a little with the anger and confusion she was feeling—waking up alone this morning, being abandoned again now. 'Sex isn't just physical, Serge. Haven't you worked that out by now?'

A muscle was ticking in his jaw and she glowered at him.

'And while we're at it, next time you decide to come into the bathroom ask before you take.'

Serge stood up slowly. 'Perhaps you should have kept the moaning down to a reasonable level, *kisa*, and then I would have heard the no.'

Visibly tensing, Clementine said hoarsely, 'I didn't say no. I just said you could have asked before invading my privacy.'

'Complaint noted,' he replied, jerking open a drawer. He wasn't indulging her temperament any further. He knew where this was going, and he didn't do female tantrums. She was being difficult for the sake of it because he was leaving her alone. Again.

Brought up short by that thought, he grabbed a T-shirt.

Yeah, okay, it wasn't the behaviour of a gentleman. But that was not what this was about. He tugged the T-shirt over his head.

What in the hell *was* this about?

He looked at Clementine as she sat on the end of the bed, tugging on the hem of that towel.

His conscience gave an unfamiliar jolt. He didn't want to leave her like this. Maybe he should cancel? Stay with her? *Bozhe*, this wasn't the way it was supposed to go. Where was the funny, happy girl he'd enjoyed yesterday?

There was something softer, more uncertain about her, and she looked genuinely upset.

'Are you okay?' he said roughly. 'I didn't hurt you? You're not sore?'

Her head snapped up and she made a little sound in the back of her throat that sounded suspiciously like a strangled scream. Clutching at the towel, she surged to her feet.

'You're a real prince—you know that?' she shouted at him, and with that enigmatic comment stalked out.

He'd never seen her lose her temper. It occurred to Serge he could have handled this better.

You're not sore?

Of all the humiliating things he could say to her—not to mention ridiculous. It told her volumes about how he saw her. Some silly girl who couldn't look after herself. Well, he had a surprise coming. She'd been looking after herself all her life, and she could deal with self-centred you're-with-me-babe men.

She yanked open drawers, slammed cupboards in the guest

room and rapidly dressed. She'd see about this *I've got to go downtown tonight.*

She had half expected him to be gone when she returned, and then she had no idea what she would have done. But he hadn't gone anywhere, and that tiny glimmer of hope she carried for this man flared a little brighter.

'If you want me to stay I'm coming with you,' she slung at him, burying her hands in her jeans' back pockets.

Serge stalled midway pulling on his leather jacket, his attention caught not by her statement but by what she was wearing. A fuzzy blue cashmere sweater which on another woman would have been casual, fade-into-the-background gear. Somehow Clementine's extravagant curves turned it into something else entirely. Something far too distracting for Forster's Gym.

It occurred to Serge in that moment that the only occasion when Clementine had actually been provocatively dressed was on that afternoon he'd followed her up the Nevsky Prospekt. Ever since she'd worn modest clothing, covering herself up from neck to knee. She didn't flaunt herself.

He hadn't considered it before, but she couldn't help being built like an old-time pin-up. A few lines of 'The Girl Can't Help It' flashed through his mind and he smiled to himself, shaking his head. He was losing his perspective if he'd started making up reasons for Clementine's sexual allure. She was a girl who could work the angles. Who knew her strengths and played to them—strengths he hadn't had enough of. Not yet.

'So don't even try arguing with me, Marinov. You really don't want to make me angry at this point,' she bulldozed on, then frowned suspiciously. 'Why are you smiling?'

Almost reflexively his eyes were drawn to her throat, where the diamond pendant was loudly not on display. Probably inappropriate, given what she was wearing, but he couldn't help but have his attention drawn to the little locket resting against the soft blue wool of the sweater.

It was a girlish locket, something clearly with sentimental value, and she seemed to be always wearing it. He had noticed that she tugged on it when she was agitated. She was tugging on it now. It bugged him.

'Apparently I've failed to make you happy, Clementine, and that's a problem.'

Damn right it was, she thought. And she wasn't going to say it was okay, because it wasn't. Shouldn't sex have brought them closer? She knew it was a naive view. Sex could mean nothing at all. But this wasn't normal. She was getting the distinct impression Serge was putting some emotional distance between them, and the message was *Burn up the sheets, but out of bed it's business as usual.*

It was probably time for some plain speaking. 'I'm not sure what's going on, Serge,' she said uncomfortably. 'You invited me to spend time with you, but I'm not spending time with you at all...' She trailed off.

His smile faded, and for the first time she saw the hard man she had glimpsed once or twice in Petersburg. 'You knew what you were getting into when you came with me, Clementine,' he said, almost formally. 'I'm making no apologies for that. I work hard. I play hard. What did you think you were signing up for?'

She shook her head in confusion. 'Signing up? I didn't know I was signing up for anything.' Then it hit her, his meaning, and two things happened. Her tummy dropped away and the chain around her neck snapped.

Clementine gave a reflexive gasp of dismay, looking down at the locket now pooled in her hand even as her head spun on the revelation this was some sort of sex date for him.

'I'll get it fixed,' Serge heard himself volunteer, unable to get over how upset she was getting, or how uncomfortable it was making him feel.

'I can take it to a jeweller myself.'

Her heart was pounding. She knew she was being too emotional, but sex had never been a casual thing for her. Deep down she'd known what he was about, but she'd jumped at the adventure of this and now she was having it. It was just she hadn't thought ahead to the consequences.

He didn't take her seriously. He might not even really like her. He just wanted to bed her.

Work hard. Play hard. Yes—what *did* you think you were signing up for, Clementine?

Silently she closed the door on the part of her that longed to be cared for and cherished, that believed she had a right to be loved—the hopeful, idealistic girl who had taken a chance in climbing aboard that jet with him. Instead she fired up the Clementine who'd been out in the world on her own for several years now—the Clementine who knew the score, who knew how to make a situation work for her.

There were two people in this arrangement. If she was having an adventure, she sure as heck was going to have some of this her way.

'I am coming,' she insisted, hands on her hips. 'I signed up to be with you, not sit around in a hotel room.' It felt good to throw his hateful words back at him. 'I'm surprised you get dates, Serge, if this is the way you treat women. Although I suppose the money helps.'

In an instant his Tartar heritage flared into life as his eyes narrowed and his expression hardened. '*Da, kisa*, the money helps.'

Somehow he had turned that insult around on her, and she stiffened, pressing her lips together. This was all going down the tube fast, and she didn't quite know how to save it.

'So what's it going to be?' she said fiercely. 'Can I come?' She couldn't quite bring herself to finish that with, *Or do I go?*

Serge pocketed his phone, his eyes travelling over her. She was a beautiful girl and she could stand up for herself. He liked it when she scratched. He wouldn't mind if she scratched harder. But it was the statement she was making with that tight, fluffy blue sweater that touched something softer inside him. For all her knowingness, Clementine really didn't have a clue.

He gave her a buried smile. 'As long as you wear a jacket, Boots.'

CHAPTER SEVEN

THE gym was a plain brick building. And Serge had been right about the sweat and testosterone. He introduced her to a man called Mick Forster, a fit guy in his fifties, who was polite but paid no more attention to her. All the other men in the room did three-sixtys as she moved through, and Clementine had never felt so conspicuous in her life. She was glad for once she had worn a neutral uniform of jeans, sweater and a vintage black velvet jacket.

She chose not to cling onto Serge's hand. She wasn't going to be the little woman on his arm. She folded her arms instead and wandered further into the gym, watching the athletes sparring, trying not to stare too long at any particular guy.

She was deep in man territory. It was nothing like her pretty pastel gym at home.

So this was how Serge had started out. Interesting.

She wandered back to find Serge deep in conversation with a group of men. She sat down on a bench. A short, strongly built young man slipped under the ropes and into the ring. A larger guy faced off with him, and Clementine watched with interest as they started feinting and jabbing, slicing the air with hands and feet. It was practice, it wasn't about breaking skin, and it was fascinating to watch how the men pulled their punches and kicks. It was a sort of masculine ballet.

She noticed no one sat down beside her. There was nothing friendly about any of these guys, but she suspected it wasn't personal. Her attention drifted back to Serge. He was talking in a low voice to Mick Forster, and they were both riveted to the sparring.

Then Mick said something, and it all happened at once. The blows made real contact. Clementine flinched as the men's bodies collided. She averted her eyes but the sounds kept coming—fist connecting with bone.

'Clementine, would you like to wait in the outer office?' Serge was bending over her, blocking her view of the ring.

She nodded, didn't argue. She felt embarrassed—and vaguely guilty.

'What in the hell did you bring *her* here for?' said Mick when Serge returned.

Serge felt an uncharacteristic surge of irritation with the older man. 'My private life isn't your business, Mick.'

'She's a distraction. You need to get your eyeline above her rack and back into the game, boy. A political move against this organisation and stadiums are going to close like mouse traps around the country.'

Serge's expression remained bland as he said quietly, but with lethal emphasis, 'If you refer to Clementine's rack again all conversations are over, Mick—you got it?'

Mick Forster rolled back on his heels. 'Well, well...' was all he said. Then, in a lower voice, 'Do you think she's up to holding your hand and being photographed at a few charity events?'

Five minutes later Serge emerged. Clementine stood up. 'Are you done?'

'We're moving, *kisa*.'

It wasn't the same as being done, but he swept her along and seated in the car she said softly, 'I'm sorry. You were right. I shouldn't have come.'

Unexpectedly he pulled her in against him, pressing a kiss to her surprised lips—a gesture of comfort. 'No, you shouldn't have come—but that was my fault.'

'Who was he? The fighter?'

'Jared Scott. We're signing him.'

'Is that good?'

'I'm counting on it, *kisa*. We're throwing a lot of backing behind him.'

'How does it work? What generates the money besides ticket sales?'

'Gambling,' Serge said flatly. 'That's all it was initially. But the organisation reached sponsorship size about five years ago. When the boys go into the ring in two weeks' time here in New York they'll be covered in logos.'

'There's a match coming up?'

'We call them events. Don't even ask, *kisa*.'

Clementine looked away. After her performance in the gym she didn't feel she *could* ask.

He didn't know why, but he felt the urge to reassure her. He'd been struggling with it since she'd sat on that bed wrapped in a towel and looking lost. But his instinct for self-preservation made him hold off. He didn't want to set up that sort of dynamic in their relationship. But this he could do.

His hand squeezed her thigh and she looked up. 'It's pretty daunting for a woman to walk into that environment. You did fine.'

It was disconcerting to realise he had read her thoughts. Yet she was beginning to anticipate his. 'Am I going to see anything of you during the day?'

'You know why I needed to come back to New York, *kisa*. It's a busy time of year for me.' Serge endeavoured to keep his tone reasonable. He'd known this question was coming. He got it from every woman he dated. They all wanted time he didn't have to give.

'It's just we've only got a week.'

Another predictable response from a woman who was proving anything but. It should have relaxed him. This should be familiar ground. This wasn't: 'How about you stay on after the end of the week?'

'Stay on?'

'After last night and today, Clementine, I'd be certifiably insane to let you go.'

'Oh.' He meant the sex. She was getting the picture.

He noticed she reflexively reached to tug on the locket that wasn't there.

'You're not interested?' He asked the perfunctory question, but of course she was.

'I have a job, Serge,' she said, her voice firmer than before. 'It was a bit of a cheek taking a week. I don't know if I could manage another.'

'Then quit.'

The nonchalance of a billionaire. Did he really think it was that easy for her? Or was it just a case of her job not meaning much to him?

'I can't just quit my job. It's a career, and it's important to me,' she spluttered. 'Besides which I've got a flat and a life to finance—not to mention it would look pretty dodgy on my CV.'

'Clementine, I don't think you understand what I'm offering you.'

She was plucking at her sweater now. Serge watched, fascinated, even as he endeavoured to work out what her problem was and exactly how much it was going to cost him.

'Two weeks in your bed in exchange for a career I've worked very hard for? I don't think so.'

'I was thinking of something more open-ended,' he said, aware Clementine was about to turn him down flat. And how in the hell he'd opened himself up to be shot down he had no idea. It was Petersburg all over again—standing in that street, feeling like a thug for upsetting Clementine, when all he'd wanted was to see her again. To go on seeing her.

Yet he wasn't quite able to get the words *I'll make it worth your while* out of his mouth. He told himself it was because he'd never actually had to say them to a woman. The women he chose to be with understood the unspoken contract: mutually enjoyable sex, a certain lifestyle made available to them, and at the end—and there was always an end, sooner rather than later—a reward in the form of jewellery or something else that softened the edges of what was essentially a sexual contract.

Or an interview in a trashy magazine. But the women who had done that were always the ones with whom he'd had only glancing contact.

Clementine looked at him with those soft grey eyes he remembered from last night.

'I don't know, Serge,' she said with quiet dignity. 'You haven't made much of an effort so far.'

Sto? A dark flush of colour moved over his high cheekbones. His male pride sat up and took notice. Not made much of an effort? What exactly did *that* mean?

'It's not as if I saw anything of you today, and after last night that felt…weird.'

'Weird?' He repeated the word as if she was speaking in another language. Something about her simple, straightforward manner was riffling through his hard-won masculine detachment.

'I felt a bit…used,' she confessed.

He shifted beside her, his eyes narowing. Clementine viewed the change in him warily.

'What is it you require, Clementine?'

He spoke so formally, his accent thickening attractively on her name.

'Time. With you.'

She asked for the moon, he thought, challenged all the same.

Diamonds were so much easier.

Yet a wild sort of certainty about how this would play out focussed him on the one thing she seemed to be asking for that he could give her.

Time in his bed. Time with him. Time for both of them.

Clementine wondered what his silence meant. She could read him a little now, but she wasn't that good.

'Serge?'

A slow, elemental smile lit up that mouth she had longed to soften with hers the very first time she'd met him.

Never had she felt like this with a man before. From the very start he had lit something inside her. She felt like a woman when she was with him, and not a gauche girl stumbling through life. She didn't want it to end. She didn't want to give him up. But she didn't want to lose her self-respect if he only thought of her as a convenience.

'I will make time.' His green eyes had darkened. He reached for her, and suddenly she was wrapped in those muscular arms and being kissed in the way she had dreamt of being woken this morning.

Clementine was up early every morning thereafter for the rest of the week. She made sure of it. It meant she was sleeping lightly and waking often, but come six a.m., when Serge stirred, her eyes were open and she was waiting for him.

She would steal her arms around his neck and hold onto him, talk drowsily about what she had planned for the day: a gallery, a ride downtown, a walk through Central Park. Serge would listen, and gradually she'd eke out a little of what he would be doing. She gathered he wasn't used to explaining himself, but he was making a manful effort on her behalf. It was a start.

On the Friday, lack of sleep caught up with her. It was light on her face that woke her, and she surfaced to an empty bed. Her heart sank. Because it told her what she'd been steadily avoiding since that first morning after: this wasn't the beginning of a relationship, it was a sexual fling.

People had them. She had girlfriends who slept with men for no other purpose than sexual enjoyment. It was a natural part of life. Apparently.

But she didn't. She had relationship sex—the sort that had a framework of mutual caring and a view to a future together. That both of her relationships had been ended by her, neither truly touching her heart, did not make it any less true. She had gone into them with an innocence, a belief in love, until Joe Carnegie showed her exactly how base the relations between men and women could be.

And that experience haunted her. She hadn't realised how much until she'd met Serge. It hung over her like Damocles' sword. She was frightened of giving too much of herself to him, of opening herself up and having Serge reduce it to something sordid.

She thought she knew him—he was sweet and generous and attentive—but waking up alone now, as she had on that first morning, brought it back to her. How they had met, where they were now—in a swish hotel, with him continuing on with his working life, her life on hiatus.

Sitting up, she looked dismally around the room.

She never got over the luxury. But it felt empty without him, and worse, it made her feel uneasy. After all, it wasn't as if they actually had a proper relationship.

The half-open door came wide and Serge wandered in with two coffee mugs, his eyes settling on her. 'You're awake, *dushka*.'

'Serge.' She couldn't hide her pleasure at seeing him.

'Cover yourself up, or I won't be responsible for my actions. And we have to move. I'm taking you to the Hamptons for the weekend.'

'Now?'

His gaze settled on her naked body. 'You're purposefully making this difficult. *Da*—now.'

Clementine leapt out of bed and ran for the door.

Serge watched her bottom wobble tantalisingly out of view. He liked waking up in the morning with Clementine warm and sweet, draped across him, and he wasn't about to pretend even to himself that he didn't; he even got a kick out of phoning her during the day and hearing that breathless 'Serge', as if she couldn't believe he had called her and would drop everything to fly to his side. Which she never did. Not Miss Independent. For all her demonstrative shows of affection he had a sense of her hovering like a butterfly, not quite sure of her perch. The analogy was apt—delicate, whimsical, difficult to hold. Her elusiveness remained, despite the week they had spent together.

It probably explained her hold over him.

It was clearer to him than ever that being a girl on call to a rich man was not a scenario Clementine truly understood. He was beginning to suspect he was her first foray into this world. If her wide-eyed reaction to the penthouse suite hadn't told him that, her refusal to wear the diamond necklace confirmed it.

He was beginning to suspect she had no idea what any of this was about—and that made two of them.

The helicopter ride out was thrilling. The view of the city below was like a movie. As they came in over the Atlantic

coast Clementine leaned down to take in the curling break-
ers on the beach below.

'You have no fear, *kisa*,' Serge shouted above the roar of
the rotorblade.

'I have a few, Slugger—just not of heights,' she sang back.
'Tell me that is *not* where we're staying?'

A beautiful large white house, set down beside dunes falling away to the beach.

On the helipad he took her hand in a casual gesture and led
her towards the house. 'Welcome home, Clementine.'

'You live here?'

'I'm thinking about buying it. I'm leasing at the moment.'

'What about St Petersburg?'

'Winter. When I can.'

For the first time she realised it made sense for him to
have a base in the US. It hadn't occurred to her before. His
business interests in the main were here. He wouldn't be living out of hotels.

He was just living in a hotel with her.

Unease slid through her but she pushed it aside. She was
here now. He'd brought her here now.

'Can you take me on a tour of the house?'

He gave her that flashing grin that told her he enjoyed
surprising her.

'It will be my pleasure,' he said, with a note of formality
that shouldn't have surprised her. He'd pulled out this traditional Russian male several times since she'd been with him
and it always got to her.

It made her trust him a little more—made her want things
from him she couldn't have.

Which was dangerous thinking. Just looking around this
huge, airy house she couldn't help but be conscious of the
gulf between them. He took this level of luxury for granted.
She wondered what he would say if he saw her shared flat,

with its two bedrooms and a showerhead over the bathtub? Picturing Serge in her tiny bolthole brought a wry smile to her lips. Picturing him in her bath made her laugh out loud, and he angled her a curious but amused look.

'What is funny, *kisa*?'

'I was thinking—what's a middle-class girl from Melbourne doing in a Russian billionaire's summer house in East Hampton?' she replied cheekily.

'Enjoying the amenities,' he shot back. 'It's all at your disposal, Clementine. The tennis court, pool, games room, theatre, and of course the Atlantic Ocean.'

They had reached the other end of the house and stepped out onto the deck, extending like the prow of a ship out towards the grassy dunes and the Atlantic beyond. The sea breeze lifted Clementine's hair and wrapped it around her neck.

'It's huge. You *cannot* live here all by yourself.'

'I'll use it for entertaining this summer.' He shrugged. 'And I'm not living here alone at the moment. I've got you.'

Clementine tried not to enjoy that comment too much, but she had to drop her chin to hide her smile at his words. He really was being very sweet. Ever since that conversation in the car, coming back from Mick Forster's gym, he'd been everything she needed him to be—attentive, considerate, looking after her needs. It was very easy to forget she was only here on a break.

Although he'd said he wanted more. And after a week so did she. She looked up at him, wondering how to broach the subject. It was hard for her. She'd been let down so often in the past. People wanted you around as long as you were entertaining or useful or fulfilled a function. Her own parents had taught her well. She came second, never first. Serge was making an effort right now, but she knew it couldn't last. She was already foreseeing the end of all of this, when one day she woke up and discovered she'd overstayed her welcome.

She was still thinking about it when Serge left her to go and make some calls. Even on a weekend break his work didn't stop. As she wandered around the state-of-the-art kitchen, opening cupboards, checking the cooking utensils, imagining the meals she could prepare in here, she mused ruefully that it wasn't other women she needed to worry about with Serge. It was the business that was her rival. If she was going to stay with him she needed to get a job, and it occurred to her that with the Marinov Corporation facing a huge public relations exercise in the media at the moment her skills might be put to some use.

She was tired of spruiking fashion. She wanted something to get her teeth into.

But mostly it would be nice to show Serge the smart girl wrapped in the sexy girl package.

Serge reappeared in quarter of an hour, stripped down to a pair of boardshorts and nothing else. Clementine went a bit weak at the knees, but told herself there was no way she was going to strip him naked and do anything remotely sexy with him in the kitchen, because it was broad daylight and anyone could walk in.

'How about we go for a swim, *kisa*?'

Her lustful thoughts dissolved as her face fell. 'I don't have a bathing suit.'

He winked at her. 'All taken care of.'

'I'm not wearing something that belonged to some random woman you brought here.'

For a moment Clementine fancied he was going to say something about those random women. Then he shrugged. 'I had a buyer bring in a summer wardrobe for you, Clementine. I checked your size from your existing clothes.'

'You bought me clothes?' She struggled to keep control of her voice.

'*Da*—I'm a prince.'

She searched his eyes for a hint of ownership, but he looked relaxed.

Okay, he was turning it all into a bit of a joke. She could relax into that. This wasn't about her in a designer dress on his arm. This was casual. This was just between them. This was his summer home.

He'd brought her to his home.

She needed to relax.

Then she flushed, a little disconcerted by the notion of Serge knowing her measurements.

'I'm waiting to be chastised for buying you clothes, *kisa*,' he drawled.

'You'll be waiting a long time,' she replied loftily, tossing her hair. 'But those bathers better be more than postage stamps.'

It was bliss to frolic in the cold Atlantic surf. Clementine had grown up beside the beach, and it was what she missed most living in England. There were beaches, but nothing like what she was used to at home.

Serge swam with her. He was a different man here. She'd noticed it even as the spit of land had come into view from the helicopter. He laughed with her and teased her, and seemed to have left the city and all his tensions behind.

As they strode out of the surf she felt confident enough to bring up the subject she'd been rehearsing in her mind all day.

'Serge,' she ventured, 'I've been thinking about what you said—about my staying on here.'

He tugged her closer, his gaze appreciative of the virtually transparent red bikini clinging to her wet skin.

'That sounds promising.'

'I was thinking maybe I could work for you. You must have a huge PR department?'

The sexual heat was doused with a bucket of reality. '*Nyet*—no, definitely not. It's not a place for you, *kisa*.'

'What do you mean? I'm fabulous at my job.'

'I have no doubt. But you won't be working in the fight game, Clementine. Not while you're with me.'

She looked at him sadly. Why did he have to bring that up? The sense there was a time limit on everything? She wanted to forget that, to be in the moment with him if the moment was all he could give her.

'Listen.' He took her chin between his thumb and index finger. 'I can send you in the direction of any number of high-profile fashion firms in this city. Getting you a job, beautiful girl, is not a problem.'

She hadn't thought of that. His contacts. The water foamed around their feet. 'I'd prefer to get my own job, Serge.'

'Does that mean you'll stay, *kisa*?' He slid his hands behind her shoulders.

She tossed her ponytail. 'I could be persuaded.'

He had her. Serge tried to ignore the rush of hot excitement that thought brought with it. Any other woman arranging her life to suit his would have rung serious warning bells, but he wanted this. He didn't want Clementine going back to London. He needed her a little longer—just until this craving for her was worked out of his system in increasingly inventive sex.

Except it hadn't been particularly inventive. His imagination came up with the scenarios, but the reality was that when she was in his arms he found it became much more about losing themselves in one another, in the kissing, the touching, but especially her soft touch. She didn't display any skills, or even really initiate anything between them. Not that he gave her much time to. He couldn't get enough of her, and the only thing that slowed him down was the impression Clementine was still adapting to him and the realities of their sexual relationship. Sometimes she would have a vulnerable look on her face, and instead of stripping her naked he would just cuddle with her—which, he told himself, proved nothing except that he was sensitive to her needs, and that made her more susceptible to future approaches.

That night the sex was fast and furious and then finished. Clementine fell into a deep sleep almost immediately it was over.

He'd worn her out. The thought stroked a male ego he hadn't known needed stroking. Yet he lay awake long afterwards, with the moonlight spilling over the bed and Clementine's face illuminated in the pale light on the pillow beside him. She was the most beautiful woman he had ever seen. But her features were slightly irregular, there were freckles all over her body, and she had the most endearing snore. Why all of this should enhance her beauty he didn't know. Only it did.

He must have dozed, because he awoke to hear her voice soft in his ear. She was telling him things, and at first all he did was listen. How overwhelming it had been for her, arriving in London three years ago, not knowing anyone, all the trouble she'd got into, the jobs she'd endured. But always she'd kept thinking: *I can't go back. I can't put my tail between my legs and go home. There's a bigger life out in the world for me.*

He figured he was only hearing all of this because his eyes were closed. His mysterious little Clem was opening up, and he wasn't about to let the cat out of the bag by shifting an inch. He could feel her hair sliding over his arm and chest, the warm press of her breast and belly and leg. He was thinking how sweet she was, confiding in him like this.

She had run into her old schoolmate and neighbour Luke in a pub— 'You remember Luke? He was going to punch you on the nose.' And suddenly her life had started to open up. On Luke's advice she'd switched to her first good job with the Ward Agency, spruiking for up-and-coming fashion designers. Her name had got passed on until she'd landed the job with Verado.

She told him how Luke had always told her it was who you knew before it was what was you did, and how she tried to make every contact count. She had learned to work a room, learned to make the most of what she had and flirt up a storm, and as a result she'd got jobs.

Da, he got that. He'd worked out for himself the sexy-girl persona was just that—something designed to get attention. He just hadn't connected that to her working life. But it made complete sense. It was why he never got that sexy girl in his bed. He got someone better, a lot less knowing, a lot more real, sensual, genuine.

As he lay there, debating whether to roll over and get up, pull the cord on this little confessional skydive, she nuzzled his neck and he opened his eyes to look down at her.

'When I first left the army I floundered around trying out a mess of jobs.'

She gave a little gasp. 'You're awake?' She sounded dismayed.

He took in her wide, worried eyes, the heat mounting her cheeks. What had amused him, and then felt a little too much like real intimacy, now changed colour again. The urge not to embarrass her made him keep talking. About selling mechanical parts on the black market, about a failed attempt to set up a trading company, about the gym training prize fighters he'd owned, which he'd almost lost when the trading company went bust but had ended up becoming his way out and up.

'Why did you get interested in the fight game?' she asked.

'Started in the army—fighting for money. I graduated to organising matches. It's not a lenient sport, *kisa*. It's better to be behind the scenes.'

Instinctively Clementine reached up and gently touched the bridge of his nose. 'Is that how you broke it?'

'Twice. It happened a long time ago. I don't even remember the pain.'

She stroked his chest. 'I don't like the idea of you being hit.'

'I'm a tough guy, *kisa*.'

'What about your family? What did they think about you being involved in the sport? What about your mother?'

'My mother died when I was nineteen.' He spoke quietly, calmly, as if reciting facts. 'She took pills.'

Clementine lifted her head, her forehead pleated with concern.

'We'll never know if it was suicide. Possibly. Probably. Don't look so dire, Clementine, it was a long time ago.'

'Your mother?' she said softly, stroking him.

'Let me tell you something about mothers, *kisa*. Mine married young. My father was an engineer—idealistic, probably bi-polar.' He slanted her a curious look, unable to believe he was telling her all this. She had stopped stroking him and her eyes were pinned to his. 'My parents loved one another with an intensity that didn't allow any air into the relationship or any light into our family life. It was two performances of *Turandot* daily.'

Clementine stayed silent, trying to form a picture of what his childhood must have been like. He stretched, as if the telling of the tale was cramping his muscles.

'Papa stepped in front of a car one afternoon when I was ten, and everything changed. Mama remarried a couple of years later. My stepfather and I didn't see eye-to-eye and I was shipped off to military school. Before you feel sorry for me, *kisa*, it was the best place for me. I rarely saw my mother and sister after that. My stepfather made a fortune out of the fall of communism and promptly lost it—put a bullet in his head. Mama wasn't far behind him. So you see—an opera in four acts.'

Clementine was silent for a moment, and then laid her head on his shoulder.

'Yes, you are,' she said softly.

'I'm what?' he enquired in a rough voice.

'A tough guy.' They were quiet together for a long time, and then she confessed, 'I don't want to go back to the city.'

It was the closest she had come to voicing how uncomfortable she was feeling, living in a hotel suite with him.

'Room Service beginning to pall, Clementine?'

He was teasing her, but there was something else in his voice. A sadness. Perhaps a leftover from his revelations, or maybe he was just over the whole impress-the-girl routine.

'It's a bit impersonal, isn't it? I hadn't realised until we came here. Being in this house is more like real life.'

Serge suddenly felt uncomfortable, and it wasn't a familiar sensation for him. Impersonal wasn't working here for him either, in this house with the ocean pounding at their doorstep. He'd brought her here to talk terms, make definite the parameters of their future relationship, but the girl lying in his arms didn't fit those terms. He'd just shared more with her than he'd shared with all the other women he'd ever known combined.

He heard himself saying, 'How about we take on some more real life?'

She looked up. The light in her eyes smote him.

'I'm taking you back to my townhouse, Clementine. I think the whole hotel scenario has worn thin, no?'

He had a home in the city. Yet they had been staying in a hotel for a week.

For a moment Clementine's whole world tipped, and everything that had come before took on a new, harsher light. Her stomach just dropped away. 'I see,' she said softly.

'Don't see too much, Clementine,' he said quietly, and she nodded—which was about all she could do.

It wasn't personal that he had chosen a hotel to get to know her, to make love to her, she thought with a savage desperation to make this all right again, to make it nothing like Joe Carnegie, to make it all romantic and hopeful again.

But nor was it personal that he had now decided to let her into his life, she acknowledged painfully. It was just a choice he was making—probably for his own comfort. She moved fast after that, making an excuse that she needed the bathroom and locking herself inside, running the bath water strong and hard to block out the sound of her tears.

CHAPTER EIGHT

THE drive back into the city gave Clementine a chance to
process events as she watched the scenery zip by and sur-
reptitiously observed Serge, who was very quiet. He liked to
drive. She had seen that in St Petersburg. They had no room
for their luggage, of course. That was coming separately.
Clementine had only her handbag, which she jumbled through
now, trying to find some of the barley sugar she always carried around with her.

Serge glanced at the objects beginning to clutter her lap.

'What have you got in there? Buried treasure?'

'Very funny.' Giving up on her surreptitious hunt, she just
shook her bag's contents out over her lap. Ticket stubs, a pen,
bits of paper, a tissue—all dropped out, fluttered down. She
found the barley sugar. And Luke's two condoms.

'Going prepared, Clementine?'

She flushed and began stuffing everything back into her
carry-all. Then was annoyed with herself for being embarrassed.

'Luke gave them to me back in Petersburg—for my date
with you, if you must know. As if you were going to get lucky
on our first date.' She couldn't resist adding, 'You had to fly
me to a fancy hotel across the world for that.'

Serge was glad he was doing a low speed and that the car

was a fluid machine to guide, because her words had him veering towards the centre of the road.

He glanced at Clementine. 'Put your hand in my pocket.'

'Serge!'

'Go on. I won't bite.'

Rolling her eyes, but curious, she reached into his jacket pocket and retrieved a small box. She opened it.

'My locket!'

'I had it repaired.'

She hadn't looked at it since she'd slipped it into a drawer beside the bed. Serge clearly had.

Dipping her head to clasp it around her throat, she experienced a wave of affection that she felt awkward about expressing. Not now that she had a much clearer-eyed view on their relationship.

'Don't tell me it's a memento from an old boyfriend,' he said in a gravelly voice.

'I bought it for myself when I turned eighteen.' She held up her wrist. 'I got this watch for myself when I signed up with Verado.'

Serge frowned. 'You purchased these yourself?'

'Why not?' she said defensively. 'Someone once told me if you don't have people in your life to mark important occasions you need to do it for yourself.' She manufactured a grin. 'Which for me is just an excuse to shop.'

No one to mark important occasions. It shouldn't bother him but it did.

'Clementine, a beautiful woman should not be buying herself jewellery.'

She gave him a bright, dismissive smile. 'Men are always buying me gifts, Serge, I just choose not to accept them.'

His knuckles rose to prominence on the wheel. He didn't want to hear about other men. But he got the message. Loud and clear. She was thinking about the diamond necklace. He wished he'd never given her the damn thing. Given? He'd left it for her to find with a note. Thanks for your services. He didn't allow himself to look back, but this was one incident he wished he could go back and change.

Yet she hadn't confronted him over it in so many words. He knew exactly where it was. In the bedside table, on his side of the bed, untouched. As far as a statement went it was pretty loud.

'You haven't talked about your family,' he said, clearing his throat. 'I assume you have them? Parents?'

Clementine looked at him sharply. He gave her a reassuring smile and her defensiveness wobbled. She nodded slowly.

'Happy childhood?' he pressed, not sure where he was going with this but feeling a bit like a drowning man grasping at sticks.

'Not really.' She suddenly became fascinated with her hands, examining her nails as she talked. 'They divorced when I was five.'

'Brought up by your mother?'

'I was handballed between them—Mum in Melbourne, Dad in Geneva. He's a journo—war correspondent. Always chasing something, whether it's a conflict, a story, a woman.' She shrugged her shoulders, dealing privately with the mixture of anger and grief she always felt when speaking about her parents. 'Mum remarried. I've got three stepsisters but I don't really know them. I left home at seventeen and I haven't been back.'

Serge frowned. 'Seventeen is young for a girl to be out on her own.'

'It is, but I managed.'

It explained a lot. Her independence, her ability to take him on, but also that vulnerability that had been worrying him.

'So you don't miss your family?' He didn't know why he was pursuing this, only he found he needed to know more about this side of her life, and until now she had never spoken about it.

'Not much to miss,' she replied briefly, looking down. 'I was still at school when I left home. I ended up working a slew of menial jobs during the day, did school at night. I wasn't getting anywhere so I made the decision to do what so many other people my age were doing and try London. I don't regret making the move. I always felt like there were opportunities out there in the world for me, and I want to take them whilst I'm young enough to enjoy them.'

Clementine suddenly wished this conversation had never started up. Talking about her parents always stirred up painful memories. A childhood where nothing was certain, all power in the hands of two adults who seemed to be nothing more than overgrown toddlers careening out of control on dodgem cars, herself alone and unprotected between them, had given her a strong need to protect herself.

At twenty-five she knew her past was beginning to take a toll. Professionally she was fine, but her personal life had never really got off the ground and now it was dead in the water.

Until this man.

Don't see too much, Clementine.

No, she wouldn't. But he wanted to be reassured she wasn't jumping the gun. That she could be the girl he wanted. The no-strings girl. But *could* she be that girl or was the price too high?

It was time to protect herself again.

She gripped her knees, and the gesture wasn't lost on him. 'Serge, can I be frank?'

He actually looked taken aback and she almost smiled. Were there worse words you could say to a man? It always prefaced something they would rather not know.

She smiled thinly. *Lucky you, Serge, you're going to get exactly what you want to hear.*

'I'm not naive,' she continued. 'I know you live for your work. Relationships are way down on your agenda. I also know that you want to keep me out of that part of your life— you want to keep your distance. I get that you chose to take me to a hotel rather than your townhouse.'

He looked as if he wanted to say something, but she got in there fast.

'You're telling me not to get serious about any of this. I get it. I understand all you're offering is an opportunity, not a long-term relationship.' She affected a casual shrug. 'It's okay. I'm cool with that. That's what I want too.' Liar, liar, pants on fire.

Serge stilled.

This should be his moment of relief. Instead it hit him like a sucker punch.

'An opportunity?' he said slowly, turning the phrase over like a rock and observing all the nasty things crawling out.

For the first time in over a week he was reminded of the girl he'd first met in St Petersburg. The girl he'd imagined had several guys on the go, working her advantages. From their first night together the notion had been rendered laughable. For all her innate sensuality Clementine was not a practised lover. In fact she had given the impression of being swept away by her feelings. It was a big part of why being with her felt so different.

Up until a moment ago he would have discounted her claim. Yet now knowing a little about her past put a slant on his perspective. She was clearly tougher than she looked. This was a woman who had survived on her own since she was a teenager. She didn't need his protection. She didn't need coddling. She was telling him exactly what he should be celebrating hearing.

'So my finding a job makes sense, don't you think?'

He looked over at her. She flashed a bright, brittle smile. *Nyet*, nothing made sense.

The next day Clementine spent her time alone, making the rounds of several fashion labels before one bit. Her CV now had Verado's name as a calling card. All her hard work in St Petersburg had paid off. The fashion label Annelli were launching a campaign over Christmas, to brand their jeans with an up-and-coming young Hollywood actress. If she was interested in joining their team they had a job for her.

The work was in New York City. There wouldn't be a problem with her visa. It was all lining up. Yet she hesitated to take the job.

In a cab uptown she thought about what all this meant.

She wanted a lot more from Serge than she suspected he ever intended to give her. You didn't take a girl to a hotel when you had a perfectly good home across town. He had never meant this to be anything more than a no-strings fling and in the Hamptons, desperate to hold onto her dignity, she'd dismissed the depth of her feelings and given him his 'Get out of Jail Free' card.

Because she did have feelings for him—and she wasn't going to deny them to herself even as she hid them from him. And the longer they were together the deeper those feelings were growing. She so desperately didn't want to be his good-time girl. She knew the impression she had given him in St Petersburg. She had hoped he knew her better now. But a week of heady lovemaking and not much else had left her teetering on the suspicion that this was always going to be a sexual affair for Serge and little else, and his luxury lifestyle only confirmed it. Why would he want more when his looks and money could bring in beautiful women from all over the world?

He had invited her into his home now, prodded her inner voice. It was something.

But it wasn't an invitation into his life, which was clearly taken up with his business.

Which was why she hesitated to take the Annelli job. Whatever he said about her not working for him, it grew more and more appealing the longer she thought about it. Being with Serge was going to mean lots of late-night drop-ins on gyms and plenty of travel, given the far-flung nature of the sport in Europe and the States. To be in his life she needed to be in his business. She could prove to him she was much more than a warm body in his bed and that she could play with the big boys too. Maybe that was a way forward for them?

But the overarching issue was the need to keep her independence, and that meant finding an apartment of her own. Being safe meant being independent. She'd learned that lesson the hard way with her parents, and had it reinforced by her experience with Joe Carnegie. Never again would a man consider he owned her simply because of the financial disparity between them.

She hopped out of the taxi on East 64th and jogged across the road towards the line of 1920s townhouses.

Serge's house had come as a lovely surprise. It was a proper home—eleven rooms over five levels. Ridiculously large for a single man, but what interested Clementine was how unpretentious it was. Completely restored, it had an old-fashioned simplicity that told her a great deal about the man she was living with, and it was oddly comforting.

She fired up the laptop in Serge's study and called up his website, navigating her way through to the schedule of matches. She knew he would be at the match on Friday night for a couple of hours, which gave her a window of opportunity to see him in action.

He didn't need to know, and it would help her build up

a sense of how to approach him about a job. She booked a ticket on-line and shut the laptop with an uneasy feeling that she had just crossed a line with Serge. If he found out he wouldn't be happy.

Serge checked his watch and then looked at the screens in the control room. The stadium was filled to capacity, the main event would soon be underway, and he could leave and drive back into town and have a late dinner with Clementine.

He was enjoying their little arrangement. He had never cohabitated with a woman before, would have run a mile if anyone had suggested it to him. Although Clementine was quick to remind him she was effectively on holiday and that once her working visa came through things would naturally change. They weren't actually living together.

She'd said that to him. *We're not living together, Serge.*

As if he needed to know where he stood. As if she was warning him off. It was starting to get on his nerves.

And she kept talking about this apartment idea. He told her there was no hurry, but it didn't stop her talking about it...

Almost as if thinking about her had conjured her up the small screen in front of him suddenly filled with her face. The wide cheekbones, pointed chin, grey eyes fluttering as she looked around, oblivious to being broadcast on a large screen.

'Hold that camera,' he said to the tech in front of him, and leaned in.

The cameras always panned in for a pretty girl, and Clementine with her lovely face, her wealth of hair down over her shoulders, in tight designer jeans and nipped-in jacket was just that. Possession gripped him behind the neck like a vice.

She was out there. Alone.

Serge registered all of this as Alex said something about going down and showing himself in the owners' box if only to make the media happy.

'That girl,' said Serge to his minder. 'Find out what seat she's in.'

'Do you want me to fetch her, boss?'

'You do not touch her,' Serge snarled. 'I'm going down. Phone me through the info.'

Alex caught up with him as he jogged down the maze of corridors.

'I thought you were seeing some Australian woman.'

'I am.'

Seat 816 FF. She was up in the gods. He had a detail of security with him as he closed in on her. She had that tight expression on her face he recognised. She wasn't comfortable with all the noise or the people around her. Good. It might teach her a lesson.

He didn't expect the look of relief on her face when she saw him—nor did he expect his instant reaction, which was an answering satisfaction. She knew who she belonged to. Then her gaze slid by him to his security, and she frowned and looked back at him uneasily.

He didn't say a word, merely extracted her from her seat. She looked up into his eyes. 'Serge, you didn't need to do this.'

'You made it necessary with your actions, Clementine.' His voice was clipped. 'I'm sure you've got an explanation as to what you think you're doing, but I haven't got time to hear it.'

He put his arm around her. From a distance it might seem a tender gesture but Clementine knew when she was being frogmarched.

Trying to defuse the situation, she laughed uneasily. 'Geez, Slugger, what are you going to do? Arrest me or something?'

'I'm going to put you somewhere safe and you're going to stay there. I don't have time to babysit you, Clementine. This isn't a local gym and a controlled environment.'

Clementine felt a pang as she remembered her embarrassing reaction when he had taken her, on her insistence, to watch the sparring. She had interrupted his working life. His important working life. And she was doing it again—only on a grander scale.

She hadn't meant to. It wasn't supposed to be like this. If he hadn't come and plucked her out of the crowd she'd still be sitting up there, him none the wiser, nothing disrupted.

It was his problem with her, and she wasn't going to take the blame.

As they approached the glassed-in owners' box she hissed, 'Maybe if you'd just issued an invite instead of shutting me out I wouldn't have had to buy a ticket.'

'*Kisa*, if you ever pull a stunt like this again there won't be any invites. Anywhere. Period.'

And with that he pushed her in front of a group of strangers and said to the nearest woman, 'Kim, this is Clementine— Clementine Chevalier, Kim Hart.' And around they went— introductions, handshakes. Hard men and heeled-up women with big hair. Clementine felt quite demure by comparison. She wondered if anyone else could hear the edge in Serge's voice or if it was just her own private horror show. Then he plopped her down in a central seat and had someone put a glass of white wine in her hand. And was gone.

Clementine watched him leave, trying not to look too panicked. He would come back for her? What had he meant, no more invites? Had she crossed some sort of relationship line she didn't know about?

A blonde whose name Clementine had forgotten leaned forward and tapped her on the shoulder. 'So what's it like being flavour of the month?'

'Ignore her,' said another voice to her left, and the woman Serge had introduced as Kim slid into the seat beside her. 'First event?'

'Yes, I'm looking forward to it,' she responded, a little blindsided by Serge's words and then by the 'flavour of the

month' comment. Doing her best to shrug it off, she switched
on her job brain and queried, 'So what's the deal here? How
is everyone connected with the Marinov Corporation?'

Kim was the chatty type, and she seemed to have a comprehensive knowledge of the business. She rolled off the fighters' agents, the sponsors present, pointed out different key
staff, then settled into the nitty-gritty of the fighters, their
stats. None of which interested Clementine in the slightest,
but as Kim chatted she was able to look around, soak in some
of the atmosphere.

About thirty-plus people circulated in the luxurious environment of the glassed-in box, milling with drinks and
nibbles. There were little screens everywhere, with different matches being broadcast from outside the arena. Outside
the glass windows rock music was pumping, but it was only
a rhythmic thump that came to her faintly.

She was suddenly glad to be in here.

'When it gets going we wander down and take ringside
seats,' explained Kim. 'Jack, my partner, number-crunches
at the top of the tree for the corporation. Completely un-
glamorous. This is the only exciting part of his job—getting
ringside seats.'

'Where's Jack?'

'Over there.' Kim pointed him out, a rangy-looking guy
in his mid thirties wearing jeans and a jacket and somehow
contriving to make them look like a suit. Clementine knew
the type. She looked at Kim. 'Do you think I could have a
chat to him? I'm interested in how everything works.'

Serge returned to fetch Clementine for the fight. He found
her with a male audience—what was new? Two accountants
and Liam O'Loughlin, his deputy head of promotion. She'd
pushed back her jacket and had her hands on her hips, and
whatever she was saying the guys were riveted to her.

'Why can't you huddle with the girls and behave yourself?' he asked as he walked her away.

'I don't know, Serge. Maybe I get a little bored talking about nail colour.'

'That's not what I mean, *kisa*, and you know it. A third of my management team are women.'

'I know.'

He looked as if he was about to say something, but the wall of noise hit them as they stepped out of the box and there was no chance for further conversation. Serge wrapped his arm around her, instantly separating her from the world in his embrace. As she looked up she had her fifteen seconds of fame as she saw them reflected on the huge screen above the ring, and then flashing logos for sponsors, car companies, sports drinks. She tried to catch them all, but Serge was walking her fast.

The combination of lights, music and an excited crowd had Clementine's blood pumping, and she could see Serge wasn't unaffected. He might be focussed on the bottom line, but he did enjoy the hoopla on some level. She hadn't noticed it before but there was a real feel for showmanship in putting on a spectacle like this, combined with meticulous planning. Serge was a planner—she got that—but this was another side to him.

It appealed to her.

Ringside seats meant they were right on the action. This time Serge introduced her in a general way to the people sitting with them, including two famous male faces that had Clementine tugging on Serge's sleeve as they sat down.

'*Da, kisa*, it is,' he responded, sitting back and stretching out his long legs. He looked like a king on his throne, thought Clementine, highly amused.

'I'm not impressed,' she said. She was—but not for any of the more obvious reasons. Having these faces ringside was publicity. It was effectively labelling the brand. The fight game was an old one, but a rap artist and a young Hollywood actor brought a different vibe to the arena. 'Serge, how much is this costing you? Setting aside the sponsors?'

He gave her a flashing smile. 'Don't worry, Clementine. I can still afford to keep you in the style you're accustomed to.'

For a moment the volume was turned down, and all she could hear was the thump, thump as her mashed-up heart made itself known. Serge hadn't noticed a thing—his full attention was on something someone was saying to do with the match. Clementine slid her hand away from his and folded her arms. Serge didn't even notice. He just rested his forearms on his knees and sat forward.

The match was starting, but it didn't much matter any more. Serge had just made it very clear how he saw her. His feelings for her were about as meaningful as the spectacle they were enjoying tonight.

She was arm candy. She was, to quote, 'the flavour of the month'. He didn't take her seriously at all. Showing him her professional skills wasn't going to change a damn thing.

The fight started and Clementine braced herself. It was the reaction of the crowd more than the thudding contact of bodies in the ring that reverberated through her. She felt each and every time bone hit bone. She could feel Serge's attention being dragged away from the fight to her, and she kept her chin up, trying not to flinch.

Serge's arm was around her and his mouth at her ear. 'What in the hell did you come for, Clementine?'

A job description, murmured a snarky little voice, but she didn't voice it.

'I'm okay, Serge. Don't make a big deal of it.' She lifted her head, made herself look at the ring.

Serge made a sound low in his chest and stood up, startling the people around him. He had hold of her hand.

She wanted to resist, but it was embarrassing enough. He escorted her towards the exit, ignoring everyone else to get her through, his minders running ahead, clearing a path. Most people were focussed on the fight, but Clementine felt humiliated as Serge dragged her grimly away from the lights and pulsing rock music that had made him his fortune.

Serge was silent as they drove at speed out of the venue and along the highway. He barely said a word to her other than, 'Get in.' That suited her. She couldn't believe how high-handedly he was behaving.

He remained silent as they entered the house. Clementine took off her jacket and went straight upstairs. She didn't want to go to bed. She didn't want to pretend this was normal. But it was late, and there was nothing else to do, so she went into the bathroom to take off her make-up and undress. She put on her pyjama bottoms and a T-shirt—the least alluring bedwear she had.

Then she climbed into bed and sat there and waited. And waited.

He wasn't coming to bed.

Well, good. She didn't want him there. All the descriptors went flying around her head: arm candy, flavour of the month, good-time girl. Who in the heck did he think he was, implying she was with him for what he could give her financially? She was independent. She worked. She'd never relied on another person for anything.

Yet the way she had felt tonight hadn't been all bad. A part of her had liked his high-handedness, had enjoyed being the girl welded to his side. The sheer physical impact of him, his charisma, the way people leapt out of his way—she had seen it through others' eyes and she'd liked it.

He owned that world in a way she hadn't quite comprehended before. He was a man who reigned over an empire which celebrated machismo, and apart from the massive profit turnover it came with a huge element of sex appeal.

If you were that kind of woman.

Clementine lifted her hands to her hot cheeks and shook her head in amused despair. He had been drenched in sex appeal tonight, and just thinking about it was making her fidget. Who was she kidding? Everything about Serge got her going, and he knew it.

She'd been doing her best all week to keep him at arm's length, to protect herself by being the independent woman who had her own life and wasn't looking to him to offer her anything more than what he had given any other woman. She had her pride, and she'd been stuffing her own needs behind it and leading with her chin.

But now she didn't bother to hide her relief when he finally came up. Stripped down to jeans and a T-shirt, he looked like the big tough guy he was and she was honest enough with herself to admit she liked that. She liked it enough to want to shove aside her anger and hurt and climb him like a tree. Her pride kept her sitting cross-legged in the middle of the bed, but she was going to be honest with him for a change. He was a tough guy—he could take it. And so could she.

'We need to talk,' he said bluntly.

'Yes, we do,' she fired back. 'And I'm going first. Now, you listen up, Slugger. I'm much more than your current squeeze. I'm very good at my job, and your little fighting empire would be lucky to have me, and if you think my living here equals being kept by you, you've got another think coming. Okay?'

He was silent, just watching her. He didn't even blink. The atmosphere began to crackle with something and Clementine shifted uneasily on the bed.

'Are you listening to me?' Her voice quavered a little.

In reply Serge stripped off his T-shirt. As muscle and taut

male skin came into view Clementine lost a little bit of concentration.

The T-shirt dropped to the floor.

'Serge?'

'You went behind my back,' was all he said, eyes hooded, gaze resting on her mouth.

She moistened her lips, shifting a little on the mattress.

'Do you have any idea how I felt, seeing your face on that screen and knowing you were out there in that crowd?'

His voice was low, intent, and he wasn't really asking a question. He was telling her.

Clementine's heart-rate kicked up and began to gallop.

Yet for some reason she thought this was the best time to throw herself off the emotional pier and blurt out, 'No, I *don't* know how you felt, because you never talk about your feelings.'

A tight smile sat at the corner of his mouth, as if he knew something she didn't. 'Well, guess what, *kisa*? I'm going to now.'

'That's good,' she prevaricated, giving a little 'oh' as he yanked down his jeans. He was naked and he was aroused and he was palming a condom from the drawer beside the bed, and Clementine wondered just when the talking part was going to take place.

He flipped her onto her back and came down over her, pinning her with his larger body. He did it so fluidly that one minute Clementine was sitting upright, fretting, and the next she was flat on her back staring into the eyes of the man who had rescued her from those thugs in the underpass.

'Now,' he said with slow deliberateness, 'let's talk about how I feel, Clementine. How about how I felt when I saw you alone in that crowd?'

He swept her T-shirt up over her head and bent to nudge a pointed rosy nipple with the stubble of his chin.

'How about how I felt when I saw you flirting with men who work for me?'

He took that nipple deep into his mouth.

'I don't know how you felt,' she gasped, but she was getting the picture.

Her body began to sing as his hand went south under the elastic of her pyjamas, testing her readiness. She'd been ready from about the time he'd said, 'We need to talk.'

'I felt like *this*.' He stripped her of the pyjama pants and cupped her bottom. Her thighs fell open of their own accord and she welcomed him as he thrust into her, a single stunning stroke. 'I felt like this, Clementine.' And he moved inside her harder, with a single-mindedness that wound her up with him, until she felt all the anger and tension in him turning into something that overwhelmed them both.

It seemed to Clementine they lay there for a very long time afterwards, just catching their breath. Her own was coming in rapid pants as she felt the throbbing in her body subside.

What had that been about?

Serge climbed off the bed and disposed of the condom in the *en suite* bathroom. Clementine watched him as he padded slowly back to the bed. He lay down beside her and pulled her body into the shelter of his. He laid a kiss on her shoulder, saying nothing. It was then Clementine realised he hadn't kissed her mouth—not once.

Yet this had felt more intimate than anything that had come before. Wasn't he supposed to be angry? Wasn't she supposed to be too? Instead she felt closer to him than ever.

Serge pulled her in tighter. What in the hell was he doing? When he'd seen her on that monitor his only thought had been to reach her. Everything else had been blotted out but the need to keep her safe. And he hadn't. He'd shoved her up ringside and everything had come undone. It was still coming undone. She made him act rashly. He'd taken her home and acted rashly again. And he suddenly had no doubt given any provocation this rashness was going to continue. Unless he made a conscious effort to stop it.

'Is that how you felt?' she whispered, turning her head to look at him, her eyes half closed, her expression so sultry he knew they were about to repeat it all over again.

'I don't know how I felt,' he admitted in a deep voice, his accent pronounced, and something in his tone snagged all Clementine's attention away from her body, still sensitised from his touch. 'But I do know now you're safe.' His arms tightened around her.

'Yes, I'm safe, Slugger,' she and answered, and reached up and patted the big arm slung around her, sounding more confident than she felt. Inside everything was knocked off kilter. As if she didn't quite belong to herself any more.

But what did that mean? That she belonged to Serge?

CHAPTER NINE

SERGE took a coffee and his cellphone out onto the deck and stood in the cool morning light as it dappled down through the leaves above. This was his sanctuary in the city—a green garden, an oasis kept in exquisite shape by people he paid.

Having the people in his life on a payroll made everything so much easier, cleaner. Nobody's emotions got involved.

Last night his behaviour in bed with Clementine had been the opposite. Hard, messy, and very emotional. The sex as a result had been incredible. The only thing that could have improved on it was not using a condom, and the fact that he'd actually considered that thought put the brakes on any future plans he had with this girl.

He'd never once not used a condom. Ever. He didn't have the sort of relationships where that was possible.

Yet he hadn't been thinking last night—not with his head and not with his body. It was how she made him feel that had been driving him, and it had translated into the best sex of his life. He'd shown little finesse, just a need to dominate her, leave his mark. He'd taken her again, with no more consideration than the first time, and she had met him with her own scaling need, and then again, with a slower, more soothing cadence, whispering things to her in Russian he could never get away with in English before sleep claimed them.

But that first time had rocked them both, and everything

that had followed held its echoes. And he would have been blind not to see how dreamy she was this morning. He'd heard her singing to herself in the shower. Hell, he'd been humming to himself until he'd realised what he was doing.

This was all without precedent.

Something about seeing her at the show last night—her fragility coupled with her independence, the sheer chutzpah she paraded around, going after what she wanted, and his inability to stop her doing exactly as she pleased—had loosed something primitive in him.

He'd known it was there. His grandmother had told him stories about his father's legendary passion for his mother, his jealous rages, the theatrics of their marriage. He didn't remember all of it—only a father whose moods had moved from highs to lows at frightening speed. He remembered that—and a mother who had been frail and ethereal, appearing to be caught up in a drama in which she didn't quite know her lines. She had only been eighteen when she gave birth to him, and not much older than he was now when she died.

He didn't want that kind of passion in his life. He didn't want to be out of control. He needed to take a big step back. Put some air between them.

Clementine came down the stairs in her runners and cargo pants. She hadn't even fiddled with her hair this morning, just left it to its natural wave. Lipstick and mascara were her only concessions to making an effort. For the first time since she was fifteen she didn't feel she had to. She felt beautiful. Serge had made her feel beautiful. She could still feel his body stunning hers, the impact of their coming together, the tension winding tighter and tighter in him until it had given way and he had been heavy and peaceful in her arms. She'd felt so powerful—like a sex goddess. A thought which put a little smile on her lips.

She'd decided before falling asleep last night to drop the

whole 'this is your life and this is mine' front and give them both a chance. Serge had demonstrated how much she meant to him. Nobody behaved that way without being borne along on strong emotions.

The fact he hadn't been in bed when she'd re-emerged from the bathroom this morning had been the only blip on her radar. She'd wanted to leap back on him and make him prove to her all over again that she hadn't dreamt last night.

She planned on taking him market shopping with her this morning, and couldn't believe how much she was looking forward to it. Back home it was her favourite Saturday morning activity. Stock up the cupboards, have lunch out with friends, maybe see a film in the afternoon. It was the sort of stuff you did with a boyfriend.

She found him on the phone, pacing the long hall between the staircase and the kitchen. His attention was immediately with her, but he averted his eyes as he continued the conversation. She went on into the kitchen to collect the eco-bags.

As she turned around she realised Serge had blocked the kitchen doorway. His hair was all ruffled and he needed a shave. The phone was dangling from one hand.

Her hormones were jumping and she couldn't wipe the happy grin off her face.

He didn't even crack a smile. 'I'm going down to Mick's gym. I'll be back around midday.'

He looked and sounded so distant—nothing like the man whose arms she had fallen asleep in last night.

The sun slipped in Clementine's sky.

'Then I've got a team of people coming over to debrief at one.'

The sun fell out of her world, and it was in that moment as she stood there clutching the bags to her waist that she realised just how deep in she was with this man.

This man who put his job before everything—or rather had chosen to today. After last night.

'You might want to organise the day for yourself, Clementine.'

So now she knew where she stood.

It hurt. It hurt so much she couldn't bear to look at him. Part of her wanted to yell at him. *Is this too hard for you, Serge, a bit too real?* But looking at him standing there, emanating power and self-control and a level of success she couldn't even fathom, she suddenly felt horribly ordinary, with her save-the-planet hemp bags and stupid, simple morning at the market, and was glad now she hadn't had a chance to open her mouth.

He'd want her out of the way. So he didn't have to be reminded of how he had lost himself inside her body last night, had revealed a part of himself he didn't want to show. It was the only explanation she could come up with, and it made her feel about an inch high.

He didn't trust her enough to understand she would protect him. She wouldn't be reckless with his feelings.

But he was with hers. Look at him—master of the universe, and me making nice with the shopping. She looked down at the bags in her arms.

'I'm going marketing,' she said, making a hopeless gesture with the bags. 'I thought you might like to come.'

But now I know you don't.

'You know I have a shopper for that stuff,' was all he said.

It was on the tip of her tongue to say, *And I know there are women who will sleep with you for money*, but her pride was too strong. He might see her as another one of his many conveniences, but she was here because she loved him.

She loved him.

In the middle of his big state-of-the-art kitchen, with flagstones underfoot and every possible mod-con a man could want in his life, making her feel never more redundant to his needs, she realised the one thing guaranteed to break her heart.

It was just sex for him, and she began to shatter into tiny pieces.

He pulled out his wallet and in front of her started peeling off notes.

For one horrified moment she couldn't move, and then the words came out as if torn from her gut. 'I can pay for a bag of apples, Serge.' And she turned around as she said it so she didn't have to face him.

She jumped as he took hold of her hips. For a strange disconnected moment it felt as if he was going to embrace her, and instinctively her body drifted up against him as he dragged her close, all the angry heat inside of her pooling in her pelvis even as her mind shouted *no*. But he was shoving the money into her back pocket instead.

'Get yourself something nice.'

He actually patted her on the backside.

He had to know what he was doing. He had to know how he was hurting her. It gave her the backbone to walk away, clutching those bags tightly to her chest. If she had the guts she'd walk away from him for ever, but she didn't have that amount of courage. Not yet. Not after last night.

The soft reminder of who she had been earlier that morning—the happy girl who had been floating on cloud nine—manifested itself in the thought: where was the closeness and belonging and sharing? Where had it gone?

Serge wasn't sharing anything this morning except his open wallet.

It burned.

It was still burning a few hours later, as she schlepped with her bags up the steps. The boxes of groceries were on delivery, but she had carried little delicacies herself: cheeses and a French wine, and some lovely Chinese tea, and those god-awful pickled herrings Serge liked.

She'd done it all despite being arm candy.

Flavour of the month. That was her.

Carrying the groceries.

As she approached the kitchen she could hear male voices. She left the bags on the bench and wandered curiously but warily into the drawing room. Serge was on his feet. About a dozen other men were sitting and standing around the room. Expensive weekend casual was the dress code, but the guys didn't look like your typical buttoned-down execs. The atmosphere vibrated with tension, and Serge didn't look happy. Her self-pity evaporated.

Only a couple of people noticed her at first, and then like an avalanche the focus of the room turned on her, the same male interest she'd been getting since she was fifteen.

Serge glanced up. The look on his face said it all and her heart sank. She took a backward step, then stood her ground. Thirteen pairs of male eyes—all directed at her.

Serge moved to her side, introducing her to the men in rapidfire succession and then gently but inexorably leading her to the door. 'We've got a lot to discuss, Clementine. It could take a while.' His tone clearly said *make yourself scarce.*

'Fair enough.' Feeling excluded, but knowing it wasn't personal, she retraced her steps and set about piling up a few plates with bruschetta, olives, cheeses, opening up a bottle of wine.

She had an idea this was about the fallout from the Kolcek disaster, and from the conversation drifting in it sounded as if she was on the money.

A heavy-set man with tattoo sleeves on both arms peeking out of his T-shirt came into the kitchen.

Behind him was Liam O'Loughlin, the promotions guy she had spoken to yesterday. She already knew she didn't like him. He compounded it by copping a look down the front of her shirt as she picked up an empty hemp bag and began folding it.

Then another man and another strolled into the kitchen, and suddenly she was standing by the island bench surrounded by five big men, all of them clearly starved of female company if their slightly inane expressions were anything to go by.

'Is this a convention or something?' she enquired smartly, to hide her subtle unease.

'Alex Khardovsky—president of the Marinov Corporation. Serge and I are old friends.' The heavy-set guy reached over the bench and shook her hand. 'Heard a lot about you, Clementine.'

Clementine's smile didn't falter, but she couldn't help the cold trickle at the idea Serge had talked about her, wondering what he had said.

'You've domesticated Serge Marinov,' said Liam O'Loughlin smarmily. 'Many women have tried and failed.'

Clementine didn't respond. She hated this sort of drivel and she really didn't like guys who couldn't keep their eyes to themselves.

'What I heard was that you worked in PR for Verado, Clementine,' interrupted Alex.

'That's right. Lots of free golf clubs and cigar clippers.'

The men laughed. Clementine pushed a glass of wine towards Alex and began pouring a couple more glasses. She didn't bother with Liam O'Loughlin.

'So you guys are all here about that fighter who's up on assault charges, right?'

'It doesn't go away,' answered a fair-haired guy with the buzz-cut.

Here goes nothing, thought Clementine, and addressed Alex.

'Your problem is managing the fallout from that big famous trial, right? You had trouble a few years ago with the media about some of your fighters' extra-curricular activities and now it's all coming back to bite you.' She pushed the platters of food towards the other men. 'Seems to me what you need is a blanket print, cable publicity blitz, pushing what's great about the sport and taking the emphasis off this over-the-top macho rubbish. Highlight the athleticism. Maybe get some of those fighters to turn up at high-profile charity events—and not on their own. You want wives and kids in tow.'

She looked up and saw Serge leaning against the doorframe. She hadn't known she was so nervous until she realised she wasn't alone. Confidence had her straightening her spine.

'Keep going,' said Alex, grinning. 'I'm taking notes.'

Clementine blew air up her fringe. This still wasn't easy.

'Yes, well…you need to get more women into your front row. Lots of famous guys there last night, but stag. Plays up to the problem you've got with Kolcek—young guys, too much testosterone, too much money, running around disrespecting women.'

'So what you're saying is the fight game isn't appealing to soccer moms?' said Liam dismissively.

'What I'm saying is you've got a problem with a thug image, and if you're serious about changing that you need to leave the theatricality in the ring and think about projecting the reality of the business, which is professional athletes engaged in highly staged combat.'

'You wouldn't consider coming and working for us, Clementine?'

'Why, Alex…' she looked at Serge over the rim of her glass '…I thought you'd never ask.'

Serge had watched the guys, one after another, follow

Clementine into the kitchen and the hairs had gone up on the back of his neck.

It was macho posturing. Clementine could take care of herself. But he'd told himself he would just check up on her—he'd do the same for any other woman he was with. There were a lot of men in the house, and for all Clementine's confidence it wouldn't be easy for a woman to handle.

Yet here she was, one hand on an outswung hip, telling Alex exactly how he needed to run his publicity machine.

A dark voice prodded him. What had he expected? Her to suddenly go all shy and play the role of his girlfriend? He reminded himself he didn't want that. He wanted the sexy girl with no ties. Well, look—he was getting it. In spades.

Provocative. Used to male attention.

It was how she got through life. She'd told him as much but he'd never actually seen it in action.

This was a woman who had survived on her own since she was a teenager. She was tougher than she looked, than she seemed when he had her wild and pinned under him.

She looked up at that moment and caught sight of him, and he actually saw some of the tension he hadn't noticed in her body leave her. Every male protective instinct in his body stood on end. She finished her little spiel and sipped her wine and met his eyes.

And because of it he moved in to stake his claim.

'Poaching my secret weapon, Aleksandr?' Serge didn't take his eyes off her as he spoke.

Alex grinned, and all the guys stirred like cattle sensing a stampede. Liam O'Loughlin was already edging his way out through the other door.

Yeah, back off. Serge couldn't believe how proprietorial he was feeling.

'She should have been sitting in there, cutting our job in half,' said Alex, looking genuinely impressed.

'Just offering a few suggestions,' Clementine said sweetly.

Alex picked up his drink. 'There's a job offer on the table. Think about it, Clementine.' He gave Serge a conspiratorial nod. 'Serge has got my number.'

Clementine eyed him cautiously when they were alone, as well she might, but he merely said, 'Keeping me on my toes, *kisa*?'

'I don't know what you mean.'

'Yeah, you do.'

She tensed. 'What's the problem, Serge? Surprised I've got a brain?'

'I'm well aware of your intelligence, *kisa*. It's how you work the room, your entirely female skills I'm referring to.'

For a moment she looked blank, and then his meaning dropped into place. 'You haven't complained before,' she said stiffly.

'It was directed at me.' A dark demon was driving him. 'I get that you're a friendly girl, *kisa*, but I don't appreciate you showering it around.'

Suddenly the hard shell was gone, and all he could see was the utter shock on her face and the flutter of confusion in her eyes before she shut down.

'Okay—fine. Whatever.' She pushed the plates towards him, her hands visibly beginning to shake. 'Here—I've made this for your guests. There should be a delivery of groceries around four.' She knocked over a glass bottle as she bumped against the bench in her haste to get away from him. Righting it, she mumbled, 'I got those awful herrings for you—more fool me.'

For a few moments Serge didn't move. He didn't know what was going on between them. He didn't understand why seeing her surrounded by other admiring men had made him so damn jealous that he couldn't see straight. He didn't even understand why he'd left her this morning.

The herrings brought him up short for a second too. She was shopping for him?

Then he noticed for the first time the tremble in her body, her refusal to look at him. He took hold of her arm. 'Clementine.'

She swung around, and for a moment he thought she was going to hit him, but she merely yanked her arm away and he let her.

'Don't worry, Serge,' she said sharply. 'I won't be turning up at your gigs any more. I know my place. I've got it pretty clear now exactly where you see me in your life. If I didn't get it before you've spelt it out now.'

She dashed out of the kitchen before he could stop her. Not fast enough he hadn't seen the flash of tears in her eyes.

Yeah, he was a real prince. He'd finally made Clementine cry.

CHAPTER TEN

IT TOOK him ten minutes to clear the house. Alex lingered the longest, took him aside on the front steps.

'What are you doing with that girl, Serge?'

'Come again?'

'The look on your face when you came into the kitchen was priceless.'

'If you could translate, Aleksandr, it might make more sense,' said Serge dryly.

'That's right—play dumb. I saw you last night. You care about her. She's not one of those bimbo airheads on your revolving door policy, she's a savvy woman. I really might employ her, *Seriosha*, then what are you going to do?'

'Fire you.'

'Touché. You know, Mick's right. You turn up with her at a few charity events and we're cooking with gas again. How about a magazine spread? "At home with Serge Marinov and the lovely Clementine".'

'You've either lost your ever loving mind or you're looking to see stars,' commented Serge, folding his arms.

'I'm not the one shacked up with Jessica Rabbit crossed with Martha Stewart.' Alex laughed and bounded down the remainder of the steps, heading for his car. 'She had groceries, man,' he shouted. *'Groceries!'*

Serge went back inside and took the stairs by threes. The

bedroom door was half ajar and he knocked a couple of times. 'Clementine?'

He'd expected to find her spread across the bed crying into a pillow, or whatever it was women did when they were put out, but the room was empty. The bed was made—nary a crease thanks to Housekeeping.

Where in the hell was she?

In the end he found her on the roof garden. She was kneeling on the ground, pulling weeds out of pots. She barely acknowledged his presence.

'First you go grocery shopping, now you're gardening,' he commented. 'This domesticity has got to stop, *kisa*.'

'Yes, well, I don't have anything else to do. You're gone most of the time and I don't have a job. So I do domestic, okay?'

He hunkered down beside her. 'Last night, Clementine—'

'Yes, I get it, Slugger,' she interrupted. 'I overstepped the mark or the boundary or whatever it is. It won't happen again.'

Serge was silent for a moment.

'I didn't want you at the event last night because it's violent,' he said with deliberation, 'and you don't react well to violence, Clementine.'

She wanted to snap, *I wasn't talking about the match. I was talking about afterwards.* 'You put me in a ringside seat,' she protested instead, turning her head so she could look him in the eyes.

'Because you were there, and I didn't want you out of my sight. I made a bad judgement call.'

'You didn't want me out of your sight?' she repeated, trying to make sense of it.

'It's my responsibility to look after you.'

The hairs prickled on her body. She was nobody's responsibility. She looked after herself. The minute she started believing Serge was going to do that was the moment this all came crashing in—as it had this morning.

He wasn't going to protect her. He wasn't going to love her. He was just her lover. Her current lover. She was a big girl. This was the way the world worked. Serge's world worked.

'You're not my dad, Serge. You're my—' She broke off, at a loss for a descriptor. Embarrassment prickled along her neck, worse than before.

'Your father lives in Geneva,' interposed Serge smoothly, letting her know she was right to hesitate. 'Do you ever see him?'

She avoided talking about her parents whenever she could, but suddenly her father seemed like a much safer topic than whether or not Serge was her boyfriend.

'No, not for many years. We had a falling-out when I was fifteen and I've never been back. I was a bit of a handful in those days.'

'Unlike now, when you're a pussycat.'

Clementine smiled a little. 'Why do you call me kitten all the time?'

'Because you're cute and playful and then you scratch me.'

She waved the gardening fork. 'Better be careful, then. I'm armed and dangerous.'

'What about your mother?'

'She presents a breakfast TV show in Melbourne. She was never home and when she was we fought. Mum and Dad were both barely out of their teens when they had me—it's why they married—and neither of them had much interest in a baby. So I grew up with a lot of childminders and nannies and fights until I was ten, when they finally split for good. Only then the fun started. The commute. Twice a year to Geneva.'

'Not fun?'

'You're kidding? A twenty-four-hour flight by myself, and then I'd be there a week and one of dad's girlfriends would arc up and I'd be hurtling back to Melbourne again. Both of them are self-obsessed—or should I say obsessed with their careers? I decided a long time ago when I have my babies I'll be staying home with them.'

'You want children?'

'One day. Don't you?' She asked the question out of interest, without thinking of the overtones.

'No.' He plucked the gardening fork out of her hand and stabbed it into one of the pots. 'But you're right, Clementine. Kids need a stable home and two loving parents.' Then he surprised her by stroking his hand gently over her head down her back to the ends of her hair. 'I'm sorry you didn't have that.'

Nobody had actually said that to her before, and the simple acknowledgement touched something raw inside her. She bent her head, enjoying the feeling of him being there with her, stroking her, offering comfort.

'Now I get it.'

'What do you get?' she asked suspiciously.

'This fierce independence of yours.'

Clementine closed her eyes, feeling herself losing her grip on the hard realities she needed to keep at the forefront of her mind. This thing with Serge could very well be temporary. She couldn't go swooping down the romantic slippery dip as she had their first night in New York and last night, because she'd only end up by herself in a heap at the bottom.

'Come on.' He stood up, offering her a hand and she took it uncertainly. 'There's somewhere I want to take you,' he said.

'Can I go like this?' She indicated her crumpled pants and dirt-stained T-shirt.

'You're fine. I like you a bit rumpled.' He put an arm around her. 'There was one thing I wanted to say about last night. Not the fight—afterwards.'

Clementine swallowed and tried to look casual. 'Oh?'

'You asked me how I felt. It feels good, Clementine. Being with you feels good.'

He took her downtown to his charity. A brown mission building in Brooklyn, housing a recreation centre for disadvantaged children.

'We have them in every city where we have venues,' he explained as they walked together through the gym. 'Here and in Europe.'

'This would be great publicity, Serge. The best antidote to Kolcek is to show what you're doing here.'

'Yeah, Mick says the same thing.'

'Mick Forster? The guy I met at the gym?'

'*Da*, he was the first trainer who would work with me when I got to the States. I wouldn't be where I am without him. He's the best in the business.'

Serge was speaking so freely she decided to take advantage of the moment. 'So what's Mick's great idea?'

'Well, for one I stop getting papped with women falling out of their dresses outside private parties.'

Clementine elbowed him hard in the ribs. 'That's not true! *Is* it true?' Some of her sweet enthusiasm evaporated, and he noticed she put a little space between their bodies. Then, more uncertainly, 'I hesitate to ask, but what are "private parties"?'

Bozhe, this woman could bring him to his knees.

He'd better get this over with quickly. 'The business I'm in, *kisa*. There's a lot of money, illegal gambling, drugs, you name it. Although we've done our best to clean it up. And there's always women. I'm healthy, clean as a whistle. Always used condoms. But I'm not one of the white bread guys you're used to. I've seen a lot and I've done a lot.'

He was nothing like the guys she was used to. Clementine knew it was silly to be shocked. She'd seen what he did for a living. She'd seen the women at those events. She'd seen the way they looked at him. He probably had phone numbers coming out of his pockets. Even that night she was with him.

The little show she'd given him in that shoe shop, which had seemed so daring to her—women probably did things like that for him all the time. Probably much more daring things.

Serge watched the emotions flickering across Clementine's expressive face. He shouldn't have told her. He'd upset her.

She gave him that negligent little shrug she'd perfected, but he knew now it covered up a lot of insecurity. 'Still doesn't tell me what private parties are.'

'It doesn't matter.' He closed the gap between them and pushed her fringe up out of her eyes. 'That's all over.'

A wave of warmth swept through him as he looked into her anxious eyes and experienced an overwhelming urge to protect her from his past. She had a lot of swagger, but she could be incredibly sweet at times. This was one of those times. It was sitting on his 'traditional Russian male' button and not getting off.

'So what are Mick's other ideas?' she surprised him by asking. Clearly the subject of other women was not a topic she wished to dwell on. Which suited him fine. He hadn't even thought about another woman in the time they had been together.

Which brought him up short.

'You'd be Mick's dream come true, Clementine. What you said to Alex about putting a wife-and-kids gloss on things is right up his alley.'

'Is Mick married?'

'Hell, no. He wouldn't be half so good at his job if he was.'

Clementine worried at her bottom lip. 'So I guess he doesn't approve of your wild lifestyle because it reflects back on the corporation? Or at least it does now, since Kolcek.'

'Wild lifestyle? Are we not in bed every evening before ten?'

Clementine blushed and shook her head. 'Maybe,' she said slowly, 'you need a woman who's not falling out of her dress?'

Serge's arms came around her. 'How about out of her cargos and T-shirt? And might I say this is a very good look on you, Clementine?'

She rolled her eyes, and Serge experienced an upswing in mood. Things felt better between them again. Whatever had been knocked awry had been restored by bringing her here, and for some reason he wasn't going to examine too closely that tight knot in his chest was gone.

He could do this. He could do light and easy and friendly. He could do sexy sweet girl who drove him a little crazy. He could do all the things that stopped short of out-of-control passion.

'So, do you want to use *me*?' she ventured, turning up her eyes to his.

'It would be ungentlemanly to ask, Clementine.'

He was gently teasing her, but Clementine was suddenly very clear on what she wanted. This was a way to test the waters—to move the relationship in the right direction. Last night had revealed he had strong feelings, but he was clearly fighting it. Maybe this was a way to give him a gentle nudge that didn't feel too real-life. A practice run.

'I think it's a dangerous idea to couple your personal life to the public face of what is essentially a business,' she said slowly, 'but I do think Mick has a point. If you have a media profile—Serge, *do* you have a media profile?'

His mouth twitched. 'A very slight one.'

'But enough to be photographed leaving parties with inappropriate women?' She tried to sound cavalier but it came out a little stiltedly.

He actually looked slightly embarrassed. Well, good—so he should. Private parties? She could just imagine…

'Maybe it would be good for you to be seen doing a few conventional guy things. With a woman.'

'But where would we find such a woman? This paragon of virtue, good manners and incredible hotness?'

He was teasing her. That was good. That meant he wasn't backing away from her. 'I don't know, Slugger. Maybe just whistle one up?'

'You're determined to get involved, aren't you?' But there was something in his expression—something that was inviting her in.

'I want to help you,' she said, suddenly feeling a little shy—which was a new feeling for her.

She hoped he was reading her right, getting the hint. Surely he could see how much he meant to her? *Tell him*, a little voice prodded. *Tell him how you feel*.

Instead she put on her professional smile, stroked his arm flirtatiously. 'I do this for a living, Slugger, just leave everything to me.'

He put an arm around her, but she noted the caution was back in his eyes. 'We'll see.'

'Public face of the Marinov Corporation,' said Clementine, feeling rather as she had when she'd first walked into that ritzy hotel with Serge a few weeks ago: kicking like mad to stay afloat. 'It'll take some getting used to,' she confessed, glancing across the table at Alex. 'I've done stuff like this before—I've just never actually been the product.'

Alex smiled at her, all charm. 'You'll do fine. Relax.'

Mick Forster strolled into the kitchen ahead of Serge, who clearly wasn't relaxed. He vibrated with tension. Clementine wondered how she could take that down a few notches.

Mick whipped off his perennial cap as he spotted Clementine sitting at the big oak table. Serge introduced them and Mick sat down gingerly at one end, a good metre from where Clementine was curled up with a coffee.

'I hear you made a good impression on Alex,' said Mick bluntly, narrowing his into-the-wind blue eyes on her. 'Do you think you can do it in front of eight politicians and a camera crew?'

'Well, Mick, I don't know,' replied Clementine, looking at Serge. 'As long as I remember to take the gum out of my mouth I'm sure we'll be fine.'

He didn't crack even a millimetre of a smile. He hadn't been smiling since she'd agreed to do this. Was he having second thoughts? She knew *she* was.

'This is just a front up,' said Serge, folding his arms. He looked so intimidating for a moment even Clementine drew back a little in her chair. Mick and Alex both looked warily at one another.

'She has her picture snapped, I do the press conference, and then we leave. No chit-chat. She doesn't speak to the press.'

No mention of doing it this way to make any of it easier for *her*, Clementine thought a little hopelessly, then nipped her self-pity in the bud. She wasn't going down that path. She had come into this eyes wide open. It was what it was: an opportunity to help him out, an opportunity to make something of what they had between them. She wasn't giving up on them without a fight; it was just right now she felt like the only person in the ring.

'I want to be sure Clementine knows what she's up for,' said Alex slowly, as if testing the waters. 'You'll be answering questions, Serge, but she'll be facing the scrum outside.'

'*Nyet*—no paps. We go in the back way. Only legit media.' Serge spoke quietly but it had its effect. The other two men stayed quiet.

'Listen, boys, I'm aware I'm going to be a handbag tomorrow,' Clementine interrupted, straining for her voice to be unnaturally high and cheerful in the tense atmosphere. 'I look good. I don't say much. I'm flashbacking to my last job.'

Nobody laughed. Nobody even twitched.

'Nah, we *want* you to speak,' said Mick finally. 'If you don't you may as well be one of those other airhead bimbos…' His voice fell away into a taut, uncomfortable silence.

Other airhead bimbos. Clementine didn't know where to look.

Ever since she'd put the proposal to Serge, Clementine had been wondering if she was out of her ever loving mind. Now Mick had pointed out what she'd been too blind or dazzled by the notion of putting a public stamp on their relationship to face. She'd be hanging her dirty laundry out for everyone to see. Anyone who was interested in the Marinov Corporation would have some idea about Serge's sexual past. She couldn't call it romantic, and there was a huge chance she was about to be showcased as a bimbo who'd made it past round one and that was about all.

Clementine suddenly felt hideously exposed and her hands found their way into her lap, winding around one another so she had something to hold onto.

She took a deep breath. She wasn't a bimbo. She wasn't going to be considered one. And this little exercise would ensure she could keep her head held high. She could handle tomorrow.

Be careful what you wish for, Clem, she told herself under the shower as she freshened up before dinner that evening. She was going to show her skills, but not in quite the way she'd wanted. In her haste to offer herself up she'd overlooked one fundamental flaw in her thinking: this wasn't about how he felt about her; it was about what she could do for him.

She'd done what she'd sworn she would never do again. In her desperation for his love, to come first with Serge, she'd forgotten her own life lesson from her parents. People wanted you around as long as you were entertaining, useful or fulfilled a function. And right now she was doing all three. She'd rushed headlong into it in her desperation to keep what she'd had a glimpse of the other night in his arms.

God help her, she wanted this to be different from what both of them had known in the past. He with his endless string of women and she with her two unsatisfactory, half-hearted relationships.

Well, she'd ensured she was in it for the long haul now—or at least until the Kolcek furore settled down and the spotlight turned to the next media frenzy. But none of this was really what she wanted. 'Come live with me and be my significant other in order to counteract media speculation over my until now playboy lifestyle' left something of a sour taste in her mouth.

She wanted a real commitment from Serge. It was time to acknowledge that, if only to herself. Pretending to be his significant other wasn't going to achieve that.

For the first time since she'd arrived on US soil with him she was beginning to wonder if any of this was worth it. It was starting to feel as if she was running after him, and it wasn't a good feeling.

She was just getting out of the shower when she heard her phone buzzing. Heavy-hearted, wrapping herself in a towelling robe, she answered it and gave a heartfelt sigh. 'Luke!'

Serge heard her voice and continued dressing in the other room, one ear on her improved tone. She hadn't sounded so upbeat all day and it bothered him. Events had coalesced all at once: the press conference, Mick's advice—which he usually heeded to his benefit—and Clementine offering herself up, the answer to Mick's prayers. She was so damn *willing* to help out.

Using Clementine in this way—and as every hour passed

that was how it was shaping up—was going to make it more brutal than it needed to be when they severed ties.

It was time to let her know this domestic idyll was over. He'd known it yesterday morning. He couldn't have a repeat of the night before. Last night he'd found concentrating on her physical needs helped keep whatever this was between them within bounds—shifting the sex up a notch to a game of skill where the name of the game was her pleasure, not how he felt when she was soft and sweet in his arms. But he would have had to be blind, deaf and dumb not to hear the emotion in her voice as she cried out his name, or see the question in her eyes before she drifted, exhausted, off to sleep. She knew the difference now. She knew he was holding back.

But he didn't have a choice. It had never been that way with anyone before, and it could never be that way between them again.

'No, I don't know,' she said, her voice suddenly pitched lower. 'No, I haven't rented anything. I might be back. I don't know.'

His heartbeat slowed.

'It's not quite what I expected.'

She was thinking about going back to London?

Every muscle in his body went on high alert. His fingers slid away from the buttons of his shirt.

Clementine gone.

This house empty.

He stood there, his head bent, breathing steadily, deeply. He told himself it was for the best.

Usually a chat with Luke lifted her spirits, but tonight Clementine felt worse than ever. It was his questions: about Serge, about her plans. They'd made her realise she couldn't make plans because none of them involved the man she loved.

She was allowed in, but only so far with Serge. Even now

their intimacy felt forced, and all about the business. Instead of making her feel more secure, as she had hoped, putting herself forward as public girlfriend only made her feel lost. Because it wasn't true—and having your picture in the paper didn't make it so.

Worse, their emotional intimacy the night of the fight hadn't been repeated. Serge was as attentive as ever, driving her pleasure, but she felt his restraint like a slap in the face. It clearly wasn't what he wanted. It was as if now she had seen how good it could be every time he touched her was a reminder of what they no longer had.

She inhaled deeply as she advanced on the kitchen. Cooking smells. Serge had only a skeleton staff, and they were never here on weekend evenings, so she knew *he* had to be cooking.

Unable to believe it, she lingered in the doorway, just watching. He looked sensational. A male animal out of the wild and giving a good impression of being domesticated.

'You're cooking.'

'I can also make beds, sweep floors and clean toilets with a small wire brush. Army training.'

'I'm impressed—although a little put off by the toilets.'

'I thought we could eat and watch an old movie and have an early night.'

Clementine told her heart not to leap but it did.

'Before D-Day?'

'You don't have to do this, Clementine.' He was suddenly deadly serious and her heart thumped in response.

'No, I want to, Serge. I want to do this for us.' She could have cursed at the slip of her tongue. She'd meant to say *you*, hadn't she?

Serge's benign expression didn't slip. He merely handed her a glass of red wine. 'To us,' he said, clinking her glass with his, but his eyes remained cool and almost watchful.

* * *

Although she'd had a dress picked out for the occasion, at the last moment it looked all wrong.

She should be good at this. She employed this skill all the time in her job. Making people see what she wanted them to see, shifting points of view, spruiking the product. Except today the product was herself, and the girl trawling through her ad hoc wardrobe wasn't finding anything. Serge put his head in the door.

'You've got fifteen, Clementine.'

'Yes, fine,' she said distractedly, not wanting to ruin a moment of today by making them late. Serge must have some nerves. He was facing a hostile media.

He hesitated, and suddenly his arm shot out and he whipped her green dress out with its hanger.

'Wear this.'

She'd worn it on their first date and she wondered if he remembered. Probably not. Why would he? And it would definitely not do.

'Thanks. I'll be with you in ten.' She purposely turned her back on him and reinstated the green satin to its place, reached for another dress with a great deal more material.

Serge consulted his watch. He could hear Clementine rushing about, the sounds of drawers closing, doors creaking, little swear words. Something about the noise she was making, the trouble she was going to, touched a part of him he was not familiar with. *I'm going to miss this.* The thought moved through him, leaving only a troubled sense of having lost something in its wake.

But she was coming slowly down the stairs, as if the last frantic quarter of an hour hadn't happened, dressed in a yellow linen high-necked dress that skimmed her breasts and hips and fell to her knees. Without a cinched-in waist her extravagant curves looked much more understated. She was playing her role. He was suddenly glad she hadn't worn the green, it brought back memories of the sweet, elusive girl he'd followed down the embankment and he didn't want those today. If he was half the man he'd built himself to be he wouldn't entertain them ever again.

Clementine did a little twirl at the bottom of the stairs. Her fragrance wrapped around him—something with damask roses, as familiar now to him as the woman who wore it. It was in the bathroom, it was in the odd piece of her clothing he'd find lying around, and it was on his pillow every morning.

She looked up and used both hands to tug at an imaginary misalignment of his suit jacket, then smiled at him, 'I think we're ready, Slugger.'

She was so lovely she took his breath away.

But there were other beautiful women in the world—as many as he wanted. Other women with toffee-coloured hair and legs that went on for ever and grey eyes. But not soft ones. He wouldn't be caught by soft eyes again. They could get under your skin. Like now.

'Anything I need to know, Serge, before we hit the road? Any last words of advice?'

'Only that you look beautiful.' He had said it a hundred times to her since they'd met, but it was only now he noticed the way the muscles beside her mouth flicked down, as if she were momentarily cringeing before the compliment sank in completely.

Because she'd heard it from a lot of men and it didn't mean much to her any more? What meant more to Clementine was to be praised for her abilities. He knew that about her now, and he fully intended to do that when all this was over. She needed to know he appreciated everything about their time together, and he could tell her now he knew she was going home.

'Do I?' she said, looking up at him, her face open and unguarded—the way she was, he realised, when they were in bed. But there was something else in her eyes. Something almost uncertain. 'Do I look beautiful? Because I'm not really. I think it's just more make-up and confidence.'

He curved his hand around the back of her head and kissed her. Her mouth fluttered under his, surprised, cautious, before her lashes swept down and she gave way. He actually felt it, the moment of her submission, and it pounded through him like big surf.

She made him feel as if he was the only man ever to do this to her. It was a fantasy, but he was going to allow himself just a little more of it before they let one another go for ever.

And it was a reminder of why he *had* to let her go—because whatever was between them was too much, too powerful. It threatened to sweep too much of what he'd worked so hard for away.

'No other woman comes close,' he said softly against her mouth. The truth, but he forced himself to release her, put air between them. 'Clementine, do you have your passport?'

'Pardon?'

'We're not going uptown, *kisa*, I'm taking you to Paris.'

CHAPTER ELEVEN

'WE CAN'T do this. What about the press conference?' blithered Clementine as he handed her into the car. He'd barely given her the time to run upstairs and grab her passport.

'Alex can handle it.'

Clementine couldn't take her eyes off him. Why was he doing this? It was irrational. It didn't make a lick of sense.

She knew Serge. He wouldn't be running away from a confrontation. He took life on, fists swinging. It was one of the things she loved about him—his willingness to front up, take it on the chin. It was something they shared.

'Serge, I have no luggage. I have nothing.' Practical considerations began to line up as she realised this was actually real. She was going to Paris.

'You've got me, *kisa*.' And he gave her that lazy Russian male smile that told her she didn't need clothes, didn't need underwear. She wasn't going to be seeing much of Paris.

Distracted for a moment by some pretty powerful imagery, she shook her head. She wasn't going to let him get away with palming her off. 'Serge Marinov, talk to me.'

He made a dismissive gesture, as if it wasn't worth talking about. 'It's not such a big deal, Clementine. All you need to know is I have no intention of using you—now or ever. It was a ridiculous idea and it was never going to fly. Happy?'

'No—yes.' She made a frustrated noise. 'Confused is what I am. How long have you been planning this?'

'Since last night. I heard you on the phone to your friend, and I got the impression you were a little homesick, *kisa*. I thought you might miss Europe.'

'No, I—' She broke off, unable even to start that sentence, which ended in *because I love you*. She put her hand on his arm. 'Serge, what are we doing? What's going on?'

She was asking him about what this did to the boundaries of this temporary sexual relationship of theirs, and she knew he knew it.

His green eyes caught hers. 'I'm taking you to Paris, Clementine, because in two days' time it's your birthday. I thought you might like to mark it with a trip somewhere special—for both of us. Something we can remember.'

Everything had been so awful, she realised for the first time, and now suddenly it wasn't. It was better than wonderful.

Happiness bubbled up from some spring inside her she hadn't known existed until that moment. It spurted like a geyser, and she did the only thing a girl could do in that moment. She flung herself across the seat at him, wrapped herself around him and sang, 'Thank you, thank you, thank you.'

And it had absolutely nothing to do with Paris and everything to do with this dear, generous man.

Serge felt slightly stiff beneath her onslaught, but his arms enfolded her. She buried her head in his shoulder and sniffled.

'You cannot cry, Clementine, this is good news. This is fun for us.'

She drew back to frame his beautiful male face with her hands. 'Yes, lots of fun,' she agreed, eyes wet, biting her lip.

Did he have even the faintest idea how much this meant to her? Probably not. But that didn't take an ounce of specialness out of his gesture.

'You're such an emotional girl, Clementine,' he teased. 'Where's my happy, funny girl?'

'She's here.' She flung herself back into his arms. She would make an effort to be more of what he wanted. She wouldn't drip all over him. She would be absolutely herself, with her big, sincere Slugger to back her up.

This was the second hotel she'd walked into with Serge, and it was a lifestyle she could get very used to. Lavish surroundings, invisible staff making their lives feel effortless...

There were surprises everywhere for her: the view of the Plâce de la Concorde, the drawers full of slinky underwear, the *armoire* layered with evening gowns and dresses for the day. Enough for her to change twice a day for a week.

How had he come up with all this?

'Personal shopper.' He shrugged it off, watching her fingering the *eau-de-nil* silk of a sheer evening gown. With his shirt open at the collar, sleeves pushed up, hair rumpled, lounging back on the vast bed, he looked like a rather louche king, surveying all he owned.

'Put it on, Clementine, so I can take it off.'

She smiled over her shoulder at him. Slowly she began to unzip, shimmy and strip. She unsnapped her bra and worked down her knickers. She didn't turn around. Then she stepped into the silk gown. It felt cool, like water on her skin, and she shivered although the room temperature was pleasant. Slowly she turned around, having no idea how it looked on her until she met Serge's eyes. Her throat ran dry. Her pulse sped up.

He was off that bed and had her flush against him so fast all she could do was squeak, 'Don't you dare hurt my dress!' and then sigh.

They had dinner in a restaurant overlooking the Seine, with a view of the lights of Nôtre Dame. Clementine wore her dress, unscathed.

The next day they wandered through the city, visiting a few tourist sites but mostly meandering. Until they washed up on the doorstep of an exclusive jeweller, when Serge took her hand and said, almost formally, 'Allow me to do this for your birthday, Clementine.'

What could she say? It was an entirely novel feeling, being escorted into a jeweller's, being sat down and having endless pieces brought out for her selection. Everything was expensive. Walking through the door, Clementine had fancied the rarefied air they were breathing must cost at least an arm and a leg. Yet she didn't feel awkward at all. It felt amazingly special. *He* made her feel special.

In the end she chose a pair of pink diamond earrings.

Her taste was praised by the staff. Serge said merely, 'Happy?'

'Happy.' It was an inadequate word for how she was feeling, but Serge seemed content with it.

Her birthday dawned cold and a little misty—very unusual for June—but the day turned into a picture-perfect summer's day. Serge had organised a balloon flight over the Loire, and lunch and an overnight stay at a private *château* he explained was owned by friends who were happy for them to put it to some use. Clementine had ceased to pinch herself, but leaning against the stone terrace rail of a sixteenth-century *château* drinking champagne, rubbing elbows with her gorgeous Russian lover, was not something she was going to forget in a hurry. And she said so.

'I've made myself memorable, then, Clementine.' His voice was warm, as if the day had pleased and mellowed him as well as her.

'I can't imagine anything more perfect. I can't imagine I'll ever forget this for as long as I live.' She made a sound and screwed up her eyes. 'Oh, Lord, I can't believe I said that. I sound so gauche.'

The champagne had loosened her tongue. She was at the end of her second glass, Serge noted, amused.

'You sound very sweet,' he replied.

'Worse!' She laughed. 'Believe me, Slugger, no woman wants to be described as sweet.'

'Incredibly sexy, then.' He plucked the goblet from her hand and slid his hands down over her hips. 'Time for bed, Clementine.'

'It's still very early, Serge,' she teased.

'Yes, but we'll be having a long night,' he replied.

He was incredibly skilled, Clementine thought the next morning, as she ate her egg and drank her orange juice on the bedroom balcony and gazed out over the dark forest that shielded the *château* from the main highway. Once the kings of France had ridden here to hounds, when much of this pastureland had been forest. Serge had told her yesterday afternoon as they explored the grounds. They shared a love of history, along with so much else. He was the best company she'd ever had.

It all went far beyond the sex, which was skilled, but not what she wanted. Not any more. He had been almost driven last night to choreograph everything that occurred between them. *Careful* was another word that came to mind. He was also romantic in a formal sense, as if searching for ways to please her out of a catalogue of 'What Women Like'. But she knew how different it could be between them when he allowed himself to let go, to feel something other than sexual gratification. It would have been her best birthday present— she would have forgone everything else: *château*, earrings, the perfection of the day—for just a few moments when she felt once more like a part of him. But it wasn't to be, and she had no idea how to change that.

'Serge…' she said out loud.

He wandered out to join her, fully dressed in slightly for-

mal attire, as if their returning to Paris merited a modicum
of style. Clementine felt a little underdressed beside him in
her robe, hair unbrushed, but she had a pretty chiffon layered frock to wear today, and she was wearing her birthday
earrings.

Was it her imagination or was he a trifle distant this morning? He'd been up before she had even woken, and the echo
of that morning in New York had passed through her before
she'd remembered how perfect the last few days had been
and how unnecessary it was to worry.

'What is it, *kisa*?'

'Can we talk about last night?' She moistened her lips. 'It
was amazing, but—is there something I should be doing?
Something you want from me?'

Serge had gone very still. In the process of pulling up a
chair to sit opposite her, he instead pushed the chair in and
stood behind it, looking down at her. It rather put her at a
disadvantage.

'What do you think you should be doing, Clementine?'

'I—I don't know. You can just seem a little—distant sometimes—when we're together—and I want to—talk about it.'

He picked up a piece of toast. 'Yes, well, *dushka*, some
things can be talked to death. If I wanted a professional in
my bed I'd pay one.'

She took a breath. Okay, he was sensitive about this. 'I
wasn't talking about technique,' she told the salt shaker. 'I
was talking about emotions. We don't seem to connect in
that way any more.'

He made a gesture of impatience and walked back into
the room. 'You're talking in riddles, Clementine. What's the
problem? Endless climaxes not enough?'

'It's not about that.' Why was he getting angry?

She understood men could be touchy about these things,
so she stood up and went to him, slid her arms around his

waist from behind, laid her cheek against his back. He didn't reciprocate, but he didn't shrug her off either.

'Sex isn't just about an orgasm, Serge. You know that as well as I do.'

His whole body seemed to grow, harden, pull away from her, but she held on.

'*Da, kisa*—it is. Between us it is.'

And just like that the bottom fell out of her world.

'What?' She gave a nervous little laugh and her arms slid from his waist as he literally stepped away from her.

'Clementine,' he said gently, but he didn't reach for her, 'this is all very romantic—Paris, dropping out of the world for a while—but we have always had just a sexual relationship. You are an incredible girl, and I'm a very lucky man, but it doesn't go any further than this.'

'Are you breaking up with me?' The words came out in a low, hard voice she didn't recognise as her own. 'Did you bring me to Paris to break up with me?'

'Hell, no.' He suddenly looked uneasy, and the knowledge shafted through her like the blade of a sword. He *had* been going to break up with her. It was just for some reason he'd changed his mind.

But he wasn't going to love her. Ever.

'You do know this will end. Everything ends.' He closed the distance between them and took her hands in his. 'I'm not going to lie and say you don't mean a great deal to me— you do.'

She wanted to curl up in the corner of the room and die.

But her pride wouldn't let her.

'Good to know, Slugger,' she said softly. She pulled her hands free and walked back out onto the balcony. He let her go, didn't follow her. He would know she wanted to cry. He was probably used to crying women. No doubt he'd passed through a lot of them.

'Clementine, it's not over.' His voice was husky, and some part of her snatched hold of that as proof he wasn't as unaffected as he pretended to be.

'No,' she said, forcing the cheer into her voice. But it fell flat. 'I just don't like talking about it. Can we change the subject?'

'We're driving back to Paris in an hour or so. There's no rush,' he said slowly. 'I thought you'd like to go out to Versailles. I think Marie Antoinette probably appeals to you, Clementine.'

She closed her eyes. He knew her so well. Yet not well enough to know she was in love with him. If he knew that, surely he wouldn't be so cruel. Surely he would lie to her. For a little longer.

Well, she was going to lie to herself. She was going to pretend she could be with a man who wasn't ever going to love her, if all he could give her was 'a great deal'.

To mean 'a great deal' to someone was something. Wasn't it?

She knew then what she had to do. Book a flight home. It was over.

Serge was angry. He didn't think he'd ever been so angry in his life. It was that cold, settled anger that could sit in your gut for days, weeks, months. It kept him silent on the drive back up to Paris. He had a pretty good idea what was keeping Clementine silent. What had he expected? She was going to chatter and sing silly songs and trade barley sugar kisses with him as she had on the way down? He'd lost that girl for good. In an act of necessary sabotage.

Yes, his anger was of the settled kind, and it wasn't going to shift, but he could feel it growing exponentially as he navigated the pretty Paris streets in the sports car and Clementine started talking about how clean Paris was compared to

London. When she had exhausted that topic she moved on to that international conundrum the weather.

'I'd like to have some time on my own,' she told him in a *faux*-sweet tone as the valet took care of the car. 'Do you mind if I go up to the suite alone?'

It was about then the anger burst. *'Da,'* he said, 'I do mind.'

She gave him a look that could incinerate and stalked ahead of him through the hotel. He didn't hurry. The anger felt good, it felt justified, and it had nothing to do with Clementine.

She had closed the door on the bedroom and thrown herself on the bed. He kicked the door open.

'Get out,' she said shifting her legs off the bed.

'I sleep here too, *kisa.*'

'I told you to get out.' When he didn't shift she said, 'Do you know what's wrong with you, Serge?'

'Go ahead—inform me.'

'You're a male chauvinist pig. You live in another century, and it's not the last one.'

He slanted her a dark look. *'Da, kisa.* You know, I had a sixteenth-century ancestor who kept fifteen wives—a couple for each day of the week. He had no trouble keeping them in line, but I guess he just hadn't met you.'

Somewhere in there was a compliment, she thought uneasily, but it got lost in the concept of fifteen wives and the way he was looking at her. All of a sudden she didn't want to be on the bed. She felt entirely too vulnerable to him.

She knew he could overwhelm her in moments—not with his expertise, although that was considerable, but with his sheer maleness, and feeling as vulnerable as she was she didn't know how she was going to cope.

She knew she could say no and Serge would stop. But no wasn't coming, and all of a sudden the only thing that was going to work was skin on skin.

All Serge knew as he came over her on the bed was that

desire crashed through him, stronger than he had ever felt it. He was driven to possess her and he would.

His father had been this way with his mother. Scenes on scenes. Crashing doors, shouting, dramatic gestures. As a child it had been terrifying. As an adult man he had been fleeing his father's legacy—a great passion destroyed in the blink of an eye.

And right now he just didn't know what it all meant any more.

He needed the sweet hot centre of her body, how it felt driving inside her, the oblivion of reaching release, of knowing nothing but pleasure with this woman who was driving him to such extremes.

Yet as he settled on top of her and began to kiss her the kissing grew slower, deeper, prolonging this time they had together. It wasn't out of control, it wasn't frenzied, and he knew then what he had been fighting.

Not Clementine. Not his past.

Himself.

What he was capable of and the fear he wouldn't be capable of it at all.

True love—deep and abiding. As if a grand passion in all its wrenching glory was all he could have and he might mistake that for the other kind. The real stuff. But the other side of that coin held by a fearful boy was a yearning for both— to love exaltedly and to love simply and truly.

Clementine's lashes fluttered down, all the resistance going out of her. The pink colour spread across her chest, up into her face, mounting her cheeks. He tugged her hair gently free of its tie and then he had his fingers spread in the silky weight, and her hands were softly caressing his neck, down over his shoulders, his back, as tantalising as a feather. She kissed him as if it nourished her. She clung and she said his name.

He slid down her body and pleasured her with his mouth

until she was trembling, and he kept going until she peaked. Then he positioned himself and stretched her, filled her, rocking into her with gentle, slow strokes until she was murmuring incoherently and locking her thighs around him. The feel of her breasts rising and falling between them, the sweet tickle of her breath on his neck, was almost too good.

'So beautiful, Clementine,' he whispered, unable not to gaze his fill of her. 'The most beautiful girl I've ever seen.'

Her eyes spilled over with tears. He gently pressed his mouth to each eyelid, catching them with his tongue.

'Sweet Clementine,' his mouth murmured against her skin, his movements increasing in tempo.

She lifted her hips, took him deeply into her, threw her head back and made a sobbing sound as her internal muscles tightened around him. He gave way with a deeply satisfied groan, the pleasure hurtling through his body at force. But it wasn't enough. He wanted more from her. Twice more he took her as the evening wore on, absorbing the heat of her body, the scent of her skin, the clash of his body giving way to the sweet clutch of hers. Until he had her limp and quiet, breathing softly beside him.

Clementine released a ragged breath and wondered why, after the most intense sexual experience of her life, she couldn't get enough breath in her lungs. She sucked in as much air as she could and turned her head, ate up the sight of him, eyes shut, chest labouring as he caught his breath, the sheen of sweat lightly glossing his skin. He had been so generous, so passionate, so much everything she wanted. Except he didn't love her, and he wasn't going to love her.

She had been wrong all along. He had never seen her as anything different from the women who had preceded her and would probably come after her. She wasn't going to mistake his tenderness, his gentleness in the act of sex, for feelings he didn't have for her.

He rolled over, and suddenly those dragon-green eyes were enmeshed with hers. Despair gripped her. In a moment she would lose herself again in wanting this to be real. But it wasn't. Tears she couldn't repress filled her eyes, spilled over, made a mess of her face.

Serge cursed and drew her in against him. His arms were tight around her, but instead of comfort it only reminded her of what she had lost.

'Don't cry, sweet Clementine, don't cry,' he murmured.

Except those words didn't mean anything, did they? Nothing was going to change, and one day—sooner rather than later—it would all be over and her heart would be smashed to smithereens.

'Tell me what's wrong?'

'I don't want it to end,' she wept, unable to hide her true feelings any more.

His Tartar blood turned his expression wild and fierce as he caught her face between his hands. 'It's not ending. Listen to me, Clementine, nothing is over.'

For an endless moment Clementine held herself in the bright circle of his assurance, the words *But you don't love me* dying on her lips, because her next words, *And I love you— so very much*, would tear this moment apart.

She couldn't do it. She couldn't tell him how much she felt when there was nothing in him to answer it. Instead she let him draw her close into his arms and listened as he began to croon to her in Russian, his hand moving in circles on her bare back. Gradually her crying fit subsided and she lay still and broken.

She lay there for a long time, until by his deep even breathing she was sure he was asleep. It wasn't even nine o'clock, but it felt much later to Clementine. It felt like an endless day that was never going to be over.

She had faced up to this when she was a seventeen-year-old girl, knowing the only way free of the emotions tearing her apart was to go out into the world on her own and make a new life.

She was a twenty-six-year-old woman now, and it should be easier. Except it wasn't. The pain was tearing her up like the claws of a wild animal and she couldn't stop it. And the longer she lay here in this bed the harder it was going to be to get up and force herself to go.

Extricating herself as carefully as possible, she silently dressed, packed her suitcase with her old clothes, and sat down to write Serge a note on hotel stationery.

She didn't know what to say and in the end she simply wrote her name—*Clementine*. One name to add to his many. She put the note on the bedside table, pinned it down with the red jewellery case, and took a last look at his sleeping form. His beautiful male face looked so peaceful—as if he'd let go of something that had been hurting him and now all she saw was a kind of relief.

One day I will feel that way too, she told herself.

'I *will* get over you Serge Marinov,' she whispered.

But the force of her emotions threatened to overwhelm her again, because something told her she never would. Not completely.

She had to protect herself. It was time to go.

CHAPTER TWELVE

THE bright lights in the main terminal at Charles de Gaulle airport seared Clementine's sensitive vision, and she made a stop at a chemist and bought a pair of cheap sunglasses, an eye-pack for the flight and some aspirin.

As she crossed the concourse she found herself looking around for him. As she queued, as she waited, even as she went through Security she kept half expecting to hear that dark Russian voice, to turn around and tangle in his eyes again. But what good would it do anyway? He didn't love her. He wasn't going to love her. The past weeks had been a fantasy. She had been right in that little shop when she had first seen him—a Cossack out of a historical epic. Ridiculous, hopelessly romantic, it didn't stand up to the light of day. He wasn't going to chase her. Not any more.

It was truly over. It was time to get on with her life.

As she bumped along the aisle to her seat in cattle class her thoughts flashed back to the private jet, and it brought home to her just how unreal her time with Serge had been.

In less than two hours she would be on her adopted home soil and life would begin again—more or less as it had been when she'd left months before. She remembered how she had felt back in St Petersburg when she'd thought she had lost him, the little lecture she had given herself about putting her experience with Joe Carnegie behind her once and for all, getting on with her life in a proactive fashion.

But now she was finding it hard to picture her flat, had forgotten Joe Carnegie, and couldn't fathom how she was going to drag herself through the next few days, let alone get a grasp on her dreams and ambitions once more. Because she had allowed herself to dream with Serge and those plans now lay in ruins.

One step at a time, her weary mind acknowledged.

As her head touched the back of her seat she closed her eyes. The noise in the plane ceased to touch her as the emotional strain took its toll and she slept.

It was five o'clock in the morning when Clementine emerged from the airport with her luggage. She wondered how she was going to get a taxi—briefly considered phoning Luke until she realised the hour. People jostled her as she ground to a halt on the concourse, but she had a suitcase, a piece of hand luggage and a shoulder bag to deal with and only two arms. She fumbled in her handbag for her purse and the money for a coffee. She needed to take a breath before she gathered herself together and thought about getting home.

Out of the corner of her eye she saw her suitcase lifted and swung out of her line of vision. She gave a cry of, 'Hey!' before her gaze ran up six and a half feet of muscle-honed male in jeans and a jacket and a blue T-shirt she remembered that brought out the intense green of his eyes. Her shock turned to heart-stuttering confusion. Then he hauled her hand luggage under his arm and took off.

'Serge!'

For a moment shock held her immobile as he strode off. With her belongings.

'Serge!' She took off after him. 'Wait! What are you doing?' She dodged and weaved through the wave of people coming in the other direction, but she was hardly going to lose him. He stood head and shoulders above the crowd, and he wasn't in a hurry. It was just the length of those long, purposeful strides.

'Stop! *Stop!*' she shrieked, no longer caring what anybody thought of her. He'd come for her. She threw herself at his back the precise moment he ground to a halt and landed smack against those big shoulders, her hands going up to steady herself.

He dumped all her luggage and turned around, his expression so fierce she took a backward step.

'Da,' he said fiercely. 'It's good you have to chase *me* for a bit. How does it feel, Clementine, being the one on the hop? Isn't that one of your Australian expressions?'

'I don't know,' she said unthinkingly, still coming to terms with his presence. 'How did you get here?' It was the least important question that came to mind, but her brain seemed to have short-circuited.

He made a 'no importance' gesture—so like the Serge she loved, king of his own fiefdom. As if the practical considerations of life that so bedevilled the general population had nothing to do with him.

'You like to run, don't you, *kisa*? Ever since I first laid eyes on you I have been chasing you. Why would it be any different now?' His tone was almost meditative, but his eyes were charged and as wild as she had ever seen them.

'I'm not running. I've come home. The holiday is over, Serge. You made that clear. You took me to Paris to break up with me.' Her voice shattered over those words. 'The most romantic time in my life and you took it and you smashed it.'

The colour left his face as her words sank in, and for a moment she experienced a modicum of satisfaction that he understood how truly awful that experience had been for her.

Then a deep sadness began to invade her, its tendrils reaching into every corner of her body.

'That wasn't my intention,' he said, in a deep, fractured voice. 'Clementine, please believe me—it was never my intention to hurt you.'

But you did.

Her whole body was howling and he was just standing there, looking fierce and troubled and desperate.

'Go and find yourself another girl, Serge,' she said heavily. 'I'm sure there are thousands of women in New York City alone who would be happy to take my place.'

He reached for her, leaning in, and suddenly all she could see was the turbulence inside of him and something else. Something tender—something awakened by her words.

'Where do you get this from? When have I looked at another woman since I met you?'

For a long moment her heart felt too big for her chest. If only he meant a word of that. But she knew it couldn't be true. She shook his hand from her arm. 'You have a history, Serge. Do you think I was living in a bubble back in New York? Everywhere I went I heard about your airhead bimbos. This is what you're like with women.'

'Not with you, Clementine.'

'We were having sex, Serge,' she hissed. 'Sex—that's all it was. You told me that's all it was. You spelt it out. How am I supposed to feel? How am I supposed to deal with that? I don't have casual flings. I'm not built that way.'

'I know you're not.'

She shook her head, shaking out the soft, persuasive sound of his words. Meaningless, empty words.

'I'm not coming back with you, Serge. It's over.'

He caught her hand. 'No.' It wasn't a plea. It wasn't a request. It was a statement of fact. *No.*

It gave her the much needed anger to power herself up.

'Get over yourself, rich boy.' She shook his hand off. 'You're not that irresistible.'

He didn't shift and suddenly she wanted him to know how badly he'd hurt her. But she also wanted him to know he was nothing special.

'I met another guy like you, Serge, a year ago. A rich guy who thought he just had to throw his money around and everything would belong to him. He dated me for six weeks. He dressed me, he asked me to wear jewellery he'd loaned me, and then he offered me an apartment because he didn't want to slum it in my flat. The problem was he was engaged the whole time and had no intention of me being anything other than his mistress. Just another guy looking for no-strings sex with an easy girl.'

Serge was looking at her as if she'd punched him.

She took a deep breath, lowering her voice. 'Except I didn't sleep with him. Because it means something to me, Serge, when I share my body. And the only reason I'm telling you any of this is so you understand what I risked when I came with you to New York City.'

'Clementine—'

She heard him say her name but she barrelled on, full of emotion, hardly knowing what she was saying or revealing any more, and not caring.

'I didn't date for a year afterwards—until I met you and took a chance. You fit the profile, Serge. Money, charisma, the sort of guy who owns the world.' She shook her head in disgust. 'But I thought, He's a good guy. I should look beyond the outer trappings to the man underneath. But in the end, Serge, you're worse than he is because you made me believe you cared about me. All that other guy did was make a fool of me.'

Serge was silent, then he said roughly, 'You should have told me.'

'I'm telling you now. I just wanted to go on a date,' she said stonily. 'I wanted to be a normal girl for a change, who gets dated instead of propositioned.'

'I never propositioned you.'

'Sure you did. You asked me to come with you to New York and my first thought was, Great, another jerk. And guess what? I was right.'

'We ran out of time,' he said softly.

'I know. That's why I said yes. Because I thought just maybe I'd give you the benefit of the doubt. I thought you saw *me*, Serge, the real me. More fool me.'

'I do see you.' Serge touched her cheek, and when she flinched turned her face to make her look at him. 'I *do* see you,' he repeated, his finger curling possessively under her chin.

'No, you don't see me at all. All you see is what everyone else sees—sexy Clementine working her stuff,' she said bitterly. 'You made that very clear yesterday. It's about sex, you said. Just sex.'

'That is not true, Clementine. I lied to you.'

She went very still.

Serge's whole body had drawn taut. 'I didn't want to feel this way about you. My parents had passion in their marriage, Clementine, and it wiped out everything else. My father thought loving meant annihilating the other person. I vowed I would never do that, and whenever I found myself getting close to a woman I would pull back. Until you.'

His eyes softened on her. 'Everything about you has been different. From the moment I saw you in that little shop, saw that smile of yours, you invited me in. It was like being a kid again, following you down that road, and when you wouldn't let me look after you I was stumped. I couldn't leave you there.'

His green eyes, so fierce as she'd flung her accusations at him, grew tender and their gazes locked.

'I've been chasing you ever since.'

She blinked.

'I'm in love with you, Clementine.'

She felt her legs give. She sat down heavily on her suitcase and Serge dropped to his knees beside her. In the middle of an airport terminal, under harsh, unforgiving lights. But all Clementine saw was the man she loved in front of her, on his knees, declaring himself.

'Then why did you push me away?' she whispered hoarsely, not really believing what he was saying.

'Fear.'

Her chin came up. It was a huge admission for a man like Serge to make, and she met the sincerity in his eyes and believed him.

'I didn't want to be like my father,' he admitted tautly. 'I didn't want to destroy the woman I loved. But, God help me, Clementine, when I woke up and found you gone I knew I'd destroyed what we had anyway. I was exactly like my father.'

He took her hands and held them between both of his—a strangely formal gesture that shook her to the ground.

'You tell me I don't see you, Clementine, but I do. Because we're alike, you and I. I see a girl who has been on her own far too long. I see a girl who takes chances and not all of them work out.' He swayed in against her until they were eye to eye. 'I see a girl who when she gets scared runs away. I'm not going to let you run away from me, Clementine. I will chase you to the ends of the earth if I have to. I love you. I will always love you.'

He took a deep, sustaining breath, as if making a declaration of intent. 'I'm a Marinov, and that is how we love our women.'

Clementine's heart stuttered, and then began to thrum to

a deeper beat. Hope was blooming inside her and it hurt too much—because she'd been disappointed so many times in the past. People promised to love you, but love wasn't always enough. Careers and personal desires got in the way. She'd learned that with her parents.

Serge seemed to sense her reticence. He let go of her hands and reached around her waist instead, suddenly so close he was her whole world.

'I've been in hell, Clementine, because I knew I'd driven you away. At the *château* I wanted to take my words back. In the car I wanted to take them back. I tried to show you in the hotel but it wasn't enough. When I woke up and found you gone I knew it wasn't enough. I didn't give you the words you needed because I found them so difficult to say—because I knew once I said them there was no going back for you and me. It's for ever. You *do* understand it's for ever, Clementine?'

A lava-flow of emotion pushed past the hard pylons she'd erected to protect herself and she laid her hand against his chest.

Serge gazed down at her hand, acknowledging the familiar gesture.

'Please don't be just saying that,' she said.

His eyes met hers, and she was stunned by the look of blatant hope in his. He wasn't holding anything back from her any more.

'Be with me, Clementine. Love me. Be mine.'

All the breath seemed to have left her body. It would be so easy to just give in. But she wasn't a little girl any more, hoping others would give her what she needed. She knew now she had to ask for it.

'I want to know first what it would be like, being yours?' she said softly, her voice growing more sure. 'Because I value my independence, Serge.'

She gave him a little smile, and his eyes lit with such a fierce light it felt slightly overwhelming.

'I will tell you what I want,' he said, his accent thickening the words. 'I want to live with you and work beside you and fill our house with friends and family and have babies with you. I want it all. But I don't know how much you want, Clementine.'

She swallowed. 'You told me once you didn't want children.'

'Clementine, I've said a lot of things I wish you'd never heard. When my father died he left behind chaos in his wake. I vowed I'd never do that. But I'd been living a half-life until I met you. I want to live fully, in the moment, and I want children with you and I want to grow old with you.'

'I took a chance, hopping in that limo with you all those weeks ago,' she said shyly. 'I can't see why I shouldn't take another chance now.'

'Forget the limo. You came across the world with a man you hardly knew.' Serge's fingers tightened around hers as he meshed their hands together. 'But, *kisa*, you must never, never do that again. Have you any idea how dangerous it is?'

She looked at their joined hands, wondering how that had happened.

'You've never felt dangerous to me. I always feel safe with you, Serge.'

'I want you to feel safe. I want to look after you, Clementine. I don't want you out in the world on your own. It takes years off me just thinking about it.'

'Then don't think about it, Slugger.'

She drifted up against him with a little smile he recognised. He kissed her softly, tenderly, with growing depth.

She wound her arms around his neck, forged that deep physical connection she had had with him from the beginning simply through the press of her body to his. But now she knew what had been there all along—the emotional link that had been forged between them, highlighted yesterday when he had moved over her on the bed and showed her he loved her because he hadn't had the words for how deeply he felt.

Now she understood. Serge didn't always have the words, but he had been showing her all along.

He looked into her eyes.

'Will you be my wife, Clementine Chevalier?'

A whole host of feelings cascaded through her, but the predominant one was certainty.

'Yes, of course I will. Was there ever any doubt?'

Serge began to chuckle, his chest vibrating with sound.

'What's so funny?'

'Oh, my elusive Clementine—was there ever any doubt? But I have you at last.'

'You always had me, Serge. You just had to ask.'

'I'm asking, *moya lyubov*.'

My love.

Clementine's heart caught on that sentiment. Happy tears sprinkled her eyes and Serge took her in his arms and kissed her.

'Come on, Boots,' he said with deep satisfaction, 'let's find a hotel. I want to be alone with you.'

* * * * *

COMING NEXT MONTH from Harlequin Presents® EXTRA
AVAILABLE OCTOBER 30, 2012

#221 A NIGHT IN THE PALACE
A Christmas Surrender
Carole Mortimer
When Giselle Barton flies to Rome at Christmas, the last thing she expects is to be kidnapped by the demanding and sinfully attractive Count Scarletti!

#222 JUST ONE LAST NIGHT
A Christmas Surrender
Helen Brooks
One last night of heady passion with her husband is too much for Melanie Masterson to resist...but it comes with an unexpected consequence....

#223 CRACKING THE DATING CODE
Battle of the Sexes
Kelly Hunter
Poppy thought she would be safe on a desert island, until she meets the owner—and he's the most dangerously sexy man she's ever seen.

#224 HOW TO WIN THE DATING WAR
Battle of the Sexes
Aimee Carson
Helping to arrange a celebrity dating event should be easy for Jessica, but Cutter Thompson's sexy smile has her breaking every rule in her relationship book!

You can find more information on upcoming Harlequin® titles, free excerpts and more at www.Harlequin.com.

HPECNM1012

#3095 UNLOCKING HER INNOCENCE
Lynne Graham
Years ago Ava stole what was most important to billionaire Vito Barbieri—now his need for revenge is only surpassed by his desire!

#3096 THE GIRL NOBODY WANTED
The Santina Crown
Lynn Raye Harris
Jilted bride Anna Constantinides incites yet another public scandal spending three days on a desert island with the world's most notorious playboy!

#3097 BANISHED TO THE HAREM
Carol Marinelli
Until Sheikh Rakhal knows whether innocent Natasha is carrying his heir, he'll not let her out of his sight—day or night!

#3098 A NIGHT OF NO RETURN
The Private Lives of Public Playboys
Sarah Morgan
Will Lucas Jackson escape his haunting past through one night of oblivion with Emma, his innocent secretary?

#3099 PAINTED THE OTHER WOMAN
Julia James
Athan Teodarkis determines to stop the dangerously beautiful Marisa's apparent advances on his brother-in-law, the only way he knows how—*he'll seduce her himself!*

#3100 THE HUSBAND SHE NEVER KNEW
The Power of Redemption
Kate Hewitt
Cruelly discarded on her wedding night, Noelle forged a glamorous mask to hide behind.... Until Ammar returns to claim his forgotten bride.

HPCNM1012

REQUEST YOUR
FREE BOOKS!

2 FREE NOVELS PLUS
2 FREE GIFTS!

YES! Please send me 2 FREE Harlequin Presents® novels and my 2 FREE gifts (gifts are worth about $10). After receiving them, if I don't wish to receive any more books, I can return the shipping statement marked "cancel." If I don't cancel, I will receive 6 brand-new novels every month and be billed just $4.30 per book in the U.S. or $4.99 per book in Canada. That's a saving of at least 14% off the cover price! It's quite a bargain! Shipping and handling is just 50¢ per book in the U.S. and 75¢ per book in Canada.* I understand that accepting the 2 free books and gifts places me under no obligation to buy anything. I can always return a shipment and cancel at any time. Even if I never buy another book, the two free books and gifts are mine to keep forever.

106/306 HDN FERQ

Name	(PLEASE PRINT)

Address		Apt. #

City	State/Prov.	Zip/Postal Code

Signature (if under 18, a parent or guardian must sign)

Mail to the **Reader Service:**
IN U.S.A.: P.O. Box 1867, Buffalo, NY 14240-1867
IN CANADA: P.O. Box 609, Fort Erie, Ontario L2A 5X3

Not valid for current subscribers to Harlequin Presents books.

**Are you a current subscriber to Harlequin Presents books
and want to receive the larger-print edition?
Call 1-800-873-8635 or visit www.ReaderService.com.**

* Terms and prices subject to change without notice. Prices do not include applicable taxes. Sales tax applicable in N.Y. Canadian residents will be charged applicable taxes. Offer not valid in Quebec. This offer is limited to one order per household. All orders subject to credit approval. Credit or debit balances in a customer's account(s) may be offset by any other outstanding balance owed by or to the customer. Please allow 4 to 6 weeks for delivery. Offer available while quantities last.

Discover the magic of the holiday season in
SLEIGH RIDE WITH THE RANCHER,
an enchanting new Harlequin® Romance story
from award-winning author Donna Alward.

Enjoy a sneak peek now!

* * *

"BUNDLE UP," he suggested, standing in the doorway. "Night's not over yet."

A strange sort of twirling started through her tummy as his gaze seemed to bore straight through to the heart of her. "It's not?"

"Not by a long shot. I have something to show you. I hope. Meet me outside in five minutes?"

She nodded. It was their last night. She couldn't imagine *not* going along with whatever he had planned.

When Hope stepped outside she first heard the bells. Once down the steps and past the snowbank she saw that Blake had hitched the horses to the sleigh again. It was dark but the sliver of moon cast an ethereal glow on the snow and the stars twinkled in the inky sky. A moonlight sleigh ride. She'd guessed there was something of the romantic in him, but this went beyond her imagining.

The practical side of her cautioned her to be careful. But the other side, the side that craved warmth and romance and intimacy…the side that she'd packaged carefully away years ago so as to protect it, urged her to get inside the sleigh and take advantage of every last bit of holiday romance she could. It was fleeting, after all. And too good to miss.

HREXP1112R

Blake sat on the bench of the driver's seat, reins in his left hand while he held out his right. "Come with me?"

She gripped his hand and stepped up and onto the seat. He'd placed a blanket on the wood this time, a cushion against the hard surface. A basket sat in between their feet and Blake smiled. "Ready?"

Ready for what? She knew he meant the ride but right now the word seemed to ask so much more. She nodded, half exhilarated, half terrified, as he drove them out of the barnyard and on a different route now—back to the pasture where they'd first taken the snowmobile. The bells called out in rhythm with hoofbeats, the sound keeping them company in the quiet night.

* * *

*Pick up a copy of SLEIGH RIDE WITH THE RANCHER
by Donna Alward in November 2012.*

*And enjoy other stories in the Harlequin® Romance
HOLIDAY MIRACLES trilogy:*

*SNOWBOUND IN THE EARL'S CASTLE
by Fiona Harper • Available now*

*MISTLETOE KISSES WITH THE BILLIONAIRE
by Shirley Jump • December 2012*

Find yourself
BANISHED TO THE HAREM
in a glamorous and tantalizing new tale from

Carol Marinelli

Playboy Sheikh Prince Rakhal Alzirz has time for
one more fling in London before he must return
to his desert kingdom—and Natasha Winters has
caught his eye. He seizes the chance to discover if
Natasha is as fiery in bed as her flaming red hair,
but their recklessness has consequences.... She
might be carrying the Alzirz heir!

BANISHED
TO THE HAREM

Available October 16!